"You like him, don't you?"

"Like who?" Ava asked.

"Carson."

"He's a patient, honey. Of course I like him."

That wasn't exactly true. She'd disliked plenty of the people she'd operated on over the years.

"Not like that," Bella said. She tipped her head sideways. Someone had braided her bangs and then clipped them off to the side. She wondered who'd done it...and how come she hadn't noticed before now.

"Every time you talk about him your face turns red."

"It does not."

Bella nodded. "It does. And you're trying to change the subject."

Ava set her fork down. She didn't want to be having this conversation. "Finish your dinner." She glanced at the puppy at her feet. "And stop feeding him scraps."

"Mom, why don't you ever go out on dates?"

Dear Reader,

I probably shouldn't tell you this, but I have a huge crush on Ryan Reynolds. And every once in a while, when I write a book, I picture a certain good-looking actor who seems to go through life with a twinkle in his eyes and a sarcastic quip flying from his lips. So when it came time to write *Home on the Ranch: Rodeo Legend*, I didn't need to look far for inspiration. I could just picture a Ryan Reynolds type of hero, one who might seem confident on the outside, but who hid his insecurities through a wisecracking facade.

You might remember my hero, Carson, from my last book, *Rodeo Legend: Shane*. Carson is Shane's brother, but unlike Shane, Carson is a ne'er-do-well without a care in the world. His perfect little world is shattered, however, when he suffers a potentially career-ending injury. Suddenly the natural talent he'd always taken for granted might just be gone forever.

Enter Dr. Ava Moore, the polar opposite of Carson. She's worked her tail off for everything she's got, and not just to please herself, but to provide for her daughter, too. That daughter wants to learn how to ride, so who better than Carson? It'll be a good way to keep him busy and his mind off an uncertain future.

Except, neither of them figured on being attracted to one another. Both of them had their futures all mapped out. They're not about to risk it all for a chance at love...

I hope you enjoy Ava and Carson's story. And if you happen to picture a certain brown-haired actor as your hero, well, I won't hold it against you.

Best,

Pamela

HOME *on the* RANCH

RODEO LEGEND

———— ✿ ————

PAMELA BRITTON

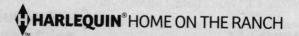

H HARLEQUIN® HOME ON THE RANCH

Recycling programs
for this product may
not exist in your area.

ISBN-13: 978-1-335-50865-2

Home on the Ranch: Rodeo Legend

Copyright © 2018 by Pamela Britton

All rights reserved. Except for use in any review, the reproduction or
utilization of this work in whole or in part in any form by any electronic,
mechanical or other means, now known or hereafter invented, including
xerography, photocopying and recording, or in any information storage
or retrieval system, is forbidden without the written permission of the
publisher, Harlequin Enterprises Limited, 22 Adelaide St. West, 40th Floor,
Toronto, Ontario M5H 4E3, Canada.

This is a work of fiction. Names, characters, places and incidents are
either the product of the author's imagination or are used fictitiously,
and any resemblance to actual persons, living or dead, business
establishments, events or locales is entirely coincidental.

This edition published by arrangement with Harlequin Books S.A.

For questions and comments about the quality of this book,
please contact us at CustomerService@Harlequin.com.

® and TM are trademarks of Harlequin Enterprises Limited or its
corporate affiliates. Trademarks indicated with ® are registered in the
United States Patent and Trademark Office, the Canadian Intellectual
Property Office and in other countries.

HARLEQUIN®

™ www.Harlequin.com

Printed in U.S.A.

With more than a million books in print, **Pamela Britton** likes to call herself the best-known author nobody's ever heard of. Of course, that changed thanks to a certain licensing agreement with that little racing organization known as NASCAR.

But before the glitz and glamour of NASCAR, Pamela wrote books that were frequently voted the best of the best by the *Detroit Free Press*, Barnes & Noble (two years in a row) and *RT Book Reviews*. She's won numerous awards, including a National Readers' Choice Award and a nomination for the Romance Writers of America Golden Heart® Award.

When not writing books, Pamela is a reporter for a local newspaper. She's also a columnist for the *American Quarter Horse Journal*.

Books by Pamela Britton

Harlequin Western Romance

Rodeo Legends: Shane

Cowboys in Uniform

Her Rodeo Hero
His Rodeo Sweetheart
The Ranger's Rodeo Rebel
Her Cowboy Lawman
Winning the Rancher's Heart

Visit the Author Profile page
at Harlequin.com for more titles.

For Dayvene.

I started listing all the reason why and it turned into a book, and I've already written one of those, so I thought, "She'll know why." But you should know my dedication has nothing to do with keeping me supplied with Fireball at horse shows. Or for traveling halfway across the country to cheer for me in the arena. Or for baking me a cake (with Fireball) and lugging it all the way to Las Vegas so we could share it with our horse show friends. And making me laugh when I can barely button my hunt coat. For being the official horse-ear-attention-getter queen of photos. But this book is dedicated to you for being a second mom to my kid. I honestly don't know what I would do without you, Dayvene. You're the sister of my heart. <3 you.

Chapter 1

"Let's see what we've got here," Dr. Ava Moore said, flipping open the cover of the tablet she'd brought into the hospital room with her and wincing at the medial epicondyle fracture she spotted on the X-ray. No wonder they'd called her in.

"Ouch." She looked up and smiled at her new patient… and nearly stopped walking.

"Is it bad?" said Mr. Carson Gillian…according to his records.

She forced a smile. "Looks painful."

Blue eyes the same color as the shallow end of a pool stared back at her, thick black lashes framing them. Dear goodness, the man could star in a beer commercial, one where he jumped off the back of a black stallion before he popped open a cold one.

And look who's being fanciful. So unlike her.

She forced her attention back on his stats. "Your chart said you injured your elbow last week?"

"Banged it on a roping chute," he admitted.

Look up. Polite smile. There.

"I'm surprised it took you this long to get to the ER." Although not really. In her experience, his type of man didn't seek medical attention unless a limb was about to fall off.

She expected a reaction to her words but he just stared down at his right elbow as if willing it to get better and, in profile, he was just as handsome. The square shape of his chin could be seen more clearly, as could what must be a day's growth of whiskers on his strong jawline. She glanced at his records again—more of a defensive reaction—and wished, for some completely ridiculous reason, that she'd worn a more flattering scrub. Horses galloping on a blue backdrop were not, as a rule, sexy, but her daughter, Bella, had insisted.

Sexy?

She refused to examine that thought too deeply.

"So, um." She took a deep breath and ordered herself to focus again. Sure, he was handsome, but in her line of work, good-looking adrenaline junkies were a dime a dozen. They were always falling off cliffs or tumbling down snow-covered mountains or doing something to hurt themselves. Like this one. She would bet he was...

She used her finger to swipe to a new page.

Yup.

Professional rodeo cowboy. Bella would go nuts. If circumstances had been different she would have loved to pick his brain about getting her daughter a horse, but now wasn't the time, not when the news she'd just imparted made him look like he wanted to vomit. Maybe in a bit, once the news had settled in.

"It's your right elbow, yes?"

He nodded. "Been killing me for a couple days now."

She could see a crease in his hair where a cowboy hat must have sat until recently. She looked around, wondering if he had any family.

Wife.

"You have a bone chip, Mr. Gillian." She forced herself to use her most chipper, professional tone. "Specifically your medial epicondyle has what's called a slab fracture. They called me in because it will need surgery if you want it to heal correctly."

When she met his gaze again she could tell he was not happy about the news. He must have been expecting it, though, because he nodded his head.

"Other doc said you might put some pins in?"

She moved forward and, for some reason, hesitated to touch him. He wore a hospital gown that exposed his elbow that, while somewhat swollen, didn't seem injured. Bruised but nothing bad. Probably why he'd taken so long to come in.

"Just one. I'll need to screw the chip to the main bone so they'll heal back together. The sooner, the better. As it stands right now I'm going to have to debride it and pin it into place and hope it heals correctly."

He tried to move the limb in question, winced. "Hope?"

"The longer an injury such as this goes untreated, the more of a risk you would be for long-term problems. Arthritis. Bone spurs. Loss of use. As such, I would recommend surgery sooner rather than later."

"You mean it might not ever work right?"

She pasted on her most sympathetic smile. "There's a chance."

His blue eyes widened. "But I'm a professional team roper."

"We'll do everything we can—"

"So I *have* to have the surgery?"

Deep breath. His kind always fought surgical procedures. "Yes. If you ever hope to regain full use of your elbow, I'll need to operate on it."

She could tell the moment it finally sank in because his eyes seemed to focus on her for the first time, like a man who'd been staring at a spot on the horizon only to note an object in the distance. She saw his brows lift a bit and though he leaned back on the bed, he seemed to straighten.

"You're the surgeon?"

"I am."

"You don't look old enough to operate on a Barbie."

She tried her best to hide her irritation. She was twenty-nine and, yes, the youngest surgical resident on the floor, but she heard it all the time and it always sort of irritated her. She didn't look her age, but that was the product of good genes and a face that didn't seem to age, not because she was young and lacked experience. It was worse when her hair was down.

"I know." She set her tablet down and reached for his elbow. "But I assure you, I'm your surgeon. You mind?"

He kept staring at her, so keenly and so intensely, heat singed the tips of her ears.

"No. Go ahead."

She tried to be gentle, but when she peeked up at him, it was as the lines on his face deepened in pain. She gently prodded his injury, feeling the tendons and muscles, and trying to gauge how securely they were attached to the bone, things an X-ray wouldn't reveal. She'd want an MRI before she operated, just to be sure.

"Were you some kind of wonder kid or something?" He had the curious expression of an engineer trying to understand a math problem. "The kind that graduated from college at twelve?"

She gently released his elbow. "Nope." And for some reason she felt the need to project an invisible barrier, forcing her most professional smile. "I'm going to write an order for an MRI. With this type of injury there's al-ways the concern that you might have some tendon damage, too. I'd like to know exactly what we're dealing with before we operate."

She could tell he didn't like the word *operate* any more now than before. He almost seemed to wince when she said the word, but that was to be expected.

"What kind of surgery are we talking about here, Doc? The kind where I'm awake, or the kind where you put me out?"

"We'll put you out. I can't risk you moving around."

He didn't look pleased by her answer. She tipped her head sideways, trying to piece together what she saw on his face. She might not have been a surgeon that long, but she'd seen his type during her residency. The pinched mouth. The furrows on his brow. The pale tint to his skin.

Fear.

He didn't like the idea of surgery. More specifically, it was tough for the alpha male to realize he wasn't infallible.

"Since it's Friday, I'm thinking we can do the pre-op on Monday and the surgery on Tuesday. Would that work?"

No, his eyes said. *I don't want to be cut on Tuesday. Or Wednesday. Or Thursday.*

That and more she read in his gaze, and it almost made her smile. Instead she did what she'd always done in these situations: she stepped forward, reached out and covered his hand with her own.

And instantly wished she hadn't.

His hand was big beneath hers, his skin warm, and she could feel fine hairs on the back of his hand, something she'd never noticed before. Not ever. Not in all her years of medical school, and certainly not since she'd started working at Via Del Caballo's general hospital.

"You'll be fine," she heard herself say as if from the

end of a long room, one where her voice didn't sound quite like her own.

"I'll take your word for it."

She let go, gave herself some breathing room. "I'll go write up that order for the MRI."

Lord help her, it was almost all she could do not to run from the room.

Surgery.

Carson tried not to think about it. He hated the thought of surgery. It reminded him of his mom…

She was back far faster than he would have thought possible, a purely professional smile on her face. Her eyes were her best feature, a shade of green that reminded him of the stones he used to pick out of a nearby lake. Jasper, it was called. Flecks of dark green and grays and browns were framed by her thick lashes. She wore no makeup, at least none that he could tell, and her lips were a little too wide for his taste, but she wasn't his type anyway. He'd tried dating a professional before. Huge mistake. He could tell the doc was a city girl, too. City girls tended to love the idea of dating a cowboy…until they caught their first whiff of a farm.

"So you ride horses?" she asked.

That was something else city women wanted to do. Ride. Until they got on a horse and realized it looked a lot more romantic than it actually was.

"Every day."

She wrote something on the tablet with a plastic pen. "My daughter is horse crazy."

Married then. Or maybe not. He didn't see a ring. "We breed cutting horses."

"Cutting horses? I have no idea what that is." She finished writing, pasted another professional smile on her face. "Part of the reason we moved here from Sacramento was so she could have a horse. She's always wanted to ride, and lately she's been interested in rodeo, too." She shook her head good-naturedly. "Haven't had time to look into getting a horse yet, though. I'm almost afraid to start. I hear it's expensive and that you really need to know what you're doing."

"You heard right."

She studied him for a moment. "You wouldn't be able to help me with that, would you?"

He tried to hide his surprise. He'd just been told he would need surgery. It took him a moment to change gears.

"I might." Actually he was pretty sure he might have a horse for her. His dad had just told him to sell a cute little mare that wasn't going to work for their program.

"My daughter's been bugging me forever. I keep putting her off, but I know I can't keep doing that." She seemed to hesitate, and it was clear she wasn't entirely comfortable about asking for a favor. "Even if you just talked to her for me. Maybe explain what's involved. We both don't know anything about horses."

"I suppose I could help out." He found the play of emotion on her face fascinating. "Maybe you could bring her out."

Her whole face lit up and it was like turning a spy glass around and seeing someone for the first time. The smile completely transformed her face.

"That would be so amazing."

Damn.

She had one of those faces that lit up when she grinned. A kind of happiness that shone from the depths of her soul and turned her into a glorious being that took his breath away for a moment.

"Probably better to do it this weekend, before I have surgery."

"Good thinking." She tipped her head, smile still in place. "I'll owe you a coffee or something."

He could think of a few ways she could thank him, but just as soon as he had the thought, he dismissed it. Buttoned-up professionals weren't his type. And for sure he could never see himself dating a doctor. She'd probably die laughing if she knew he fainted at the sight of blood, especially his own. But he didn't mind helping her out. Couldn't hurt to get in good with his doc.

"Bring her out on Saturday. Gillian Ranch. It's off the old Highway 21. You can google it."

Her eyes crinkled near the corners. "Great. I'll see you then."

Chapter 2

"Oh my gosh, Mom!"

Bella could barely sit still on the seat next to her as Ava pulled to a stop in front of a massive Spanish-style barn with a terra-cotta roof and an off-white stucco exterior.

"This place is ah-may-zing."

Ava would have to agree, a smile coming to her face at how animated her nine-year-old daughter had become. They'd driven for what seemed like forever along back roads until she'd seen the entrance to the ranch, then down an oak-studded driveway and then through vineyards until an oasis of homes and buildings and arenas had appeared. Who these people were, she had no idea, but it was clear they were wealthy.

"I'm gonna look at the horses."

"Bella, wait," she cried. But her daughter was off, dashing into the stable without waiting for Ava to get out of the SUV. "Darn it."

It wasn't like Bella to disobey her, but she supposed she could be forgiven. For as long as she'd been old enough to talk, her favorite word had been *horse*. Before Paul had died they'd had plans...

She slammed the door of her SUV because thoughts of Paul made her sad, especially on this day when one of his daughter's fondest wishes had finally come true.

"Mom, look!" Bella spun around. "Isn't this gorgeous."

The place really was. Like something out of a movie

set where a beautiful Spanish princess came to ride her steeds. The outside reminded her of a mission with its stucco exterior and red-tiled roof, but the inside was spacious and airy with wooden stalls that had wrought-iron bars across the fronts.

Movement caught her eye as someone came through the opening at the far end. The man she'd been unable to forget.

"Hey, there," Carson Gillian said.

Color stained her cheeks. She had no idea why. Perhaps because the man disturbed her on a purely feminine level that she did her best to ignore. Hard to do that with him right in front of her, though.

"Good morning," she said brightly.

Bella turned from her position near a horse's head. "Hi."

He glanced at her daughter and his face registered surprise for a moment. She wondered why.

"You must be Bella."

"I am."

He walked toward her daughter with his good hand outstretched, the cast on his elbow blending with his white T-shirt so that it looked like he was wearing a long sleeve on one arm. She'd put it on him the other day, right after she'd asked him to let her bring Bella to his ranch. He'd been strangely quiet as she'd done it.

A million times she'd told herself to back out of this visit. His invitation to Gillian Ranch had taken her by surprise, but once the offer had been made, it was hard to say no. Partly because Bella had been on her case since the move, but also because Ava was really hoping talk of horses would help distract Bella from some of the other problems she'd been having. Later, though, she wondered if she should've thought it through more. It wasn't like her to pounce on a new patient and ask for favors—a clear sign of her desperation. And once she'd told Bella about Carson's offer, there'd been no turning back.

"Do I get to ride one?" Bella asked, her long brown ponytail nearly slapping her in the face when she turned back to the horse she'd been trying to pet.

"Bella, no. That's not what we're here to do. Mr. Gillian just wanted to talk to you about what's entailed when you own a horse."

"Actually." He scratched the back of his neck. "I got to thinking about it, and we might have a horse or two that may, and I stress, *may* work out for her."

"Really?" Bella's squeal startled the horse inside the stall.

"Bella, quiet. I'm sure Mr. Gillian doesn't want you scaring his horses."

"Do you mean we might actually buy a horse?" Bella's eyes were wide. "Today."

"Well, I—"

Carson shook his head, held up a hand. "Not unless I think it's a perfect fit. And not until you learn how to ride. And how to care for a horse and clean their feet and feed them and groom them. And they're not my horses. They're my dad's and uncle's. These are their show horses. They're used to people doing crazy things. But you should still keep your cool."

Bella looked suitably cowed.

Ava tried to keep from staring at Carson by pretending an interest in her surroundings. One of the other residents had told her Carson's dad and uncle were famous rodeo riders, or they had been. Now they raised cutting horses—specialized horses used to herd cows—according to her coworker. Some of the finest in the nation. He'd encouraged her to take Bella to the ranch, which had made her feel marginally better for putting a perfect stranger on the spot and enlisting his help. And so here she was and, if she were honest, a bit reluctantly because long after Carson Gillian had left the hospital she'd thought about him, and not in an impersonal I'm-going-to-operate-on-you kind of way.

Ridiculously good-looking.

That was the thought that'd kept crossing her mind, and it was confirmed this morning as he stood there in his well-worn blue jeans that looked on the verge of blowing out in the rear section.

She blushed again.

"Thanks for letting us visit." She felt the need to say it because Bella had run off to another stall and suddenly she was alone with him and feeling more and more self-conscious by the moment.

"My pleasure." He smiled, his thick brows lifting. "Least I could do, given what you plan to do for me." He raised his wounded arm.

You've had other good-looking patients before. So what's different about this one?

But she knew the answer to that, and she'd known it that day in the hospital. He reminded her of Paul. It wasn't just his good looks. It was his rugged masculinity. It was the way he carried himself. Because even sitting in a hospital bed he'd had the air of a man who did what he wanted to do and damn how his loved ones felt about it. A man to avoid. She'd learned that lesson the hard way.

"What's this one's name?" Bella called, peeking between horizontal round bars that kept the horse from peeking out. "He's so pretty."

"*She* is called Flashy." Carson's smile grew. "For obvious reasons."

They paused outside the horse's stall and Carson

moved forward to open a tiny door in the upper half. The horse immediately poked her head out, her long blond mane touching the rim of the opening, her kind brown eyes fixed on Bella.

"Wow," Ava said. "That mane makes her the female Fabio of horses, doesn't it?"

Carson smiled. "Thus, the name Flashy."

"Can I pet her?" Bella asked.

"Of course."

Bella seemed in awe and it softened Ava's discomfort as she caught the joy in her daughter's eyes. She'd worn her "riding outfit" today, a pair of beige tights that she said looked just like riding breeches on TV and a pair of Western boots. Her favorite shirt, one that was getting too small but that featured the head of the animal she loved amid a white backdrop, hugged her little-girl body. She'd pulled her brown hair back into a ponytail. It showed off her profile and her little button nose, which sat beneath brown eyes. Based on the smile on her face, she was blissfully, completely, entranced with her surroundings.

Okay, so maybe petitioning a patient for help wasn't such a bad idea after all.

Ava moved up to the horse, holding out a hand. "She's a beautiful animal." She met Bella's gaze and smiled.

"Isn't she, Mom? I love her."

"She's one of the best horses in the barn," Carson said. "Never cheats a rider. Always gives you her all. We plan to breed her when she's done showing."

"Neat," Bella cooed.

Ava took a deep breath and told herself to relax. This was going to be so great for her daughter. It was just what they needed.

"How many horses do you have here?" Ava asked.

"Me, personally?" Carson asked. "Two. I rope off them."

"But not now," said the doctor in her.

"No." He shook his head. "We have about twenty-five on-site. It's a lot of work, which is something I meant to ask you about the other day. How soon after surgery will I be able to ride again?"

She saw it then…a hint of worry in his eyes. She'd seen that same look on his face at the hospital, and on other faces throughout the years, and not just on the professional athletes. She said the same thing she always said: "Not until after the bones are fully knitted, and definitely not until after some therapy."

He seemed disappointed by her answer. That, too, was par for the course.

"Look, I know it's tough to suddenly slow down—"

"You have no idea."

Actually she did after watching so many patients go through it. "You have to give it time, but I have no doubt you'll be back in the saddle one day soon."

"What happened to you?" Bella asked, concern on her face. She was always so worried about everyone else, probably because of her own loss early in life.

"I was coming out of the roping chute and my horse hit the barrier so hard he tripped."

"Barrier?" Bella asked.

"It's a rope that hangs across the front of a roping chute. It keeps a horse and rider back while the steer has time to run out."

Bella nodded. Ava smiled, hoping she never lost her curiosity about the unknown.

"Somehow I ended up coming off. Banged my elbow on the chute, although I don't know how. I must have twisted or something when I fell."

"So my mom's going to operate on it?" Bella asked.

Carson nodded. "Hoping it'll be as good as new."

Bella reached for his arm, the good one, resting her fingers on it. "I hope so, too, Mr. Gillian."

It was such a kindhearted thing to do, it made Ava's heart swell with pride. Maybe she wasn't such a bad parent after all, although it sometimes felt that way with the hours she worked.

When she glanced at Carson, it was in time to see him staring down at Bella in bemusement. "Like mother, like daughter."

Damn her fair complexion. Did he see the way her cheeks filled with color again? She pretended an interest in her turquoise-colored shirt, plucking at an imaginary string.

"Mr. Gillian, can I see the horse I'm going to ride?" Bella smiled up at him.

"Sure." Carson stepped away, so quickly Ava wondered if maybe he had spotted her embarrassment, or if, horror upon horrors, he somehow knew she'd been thinking about him nonstop. "I'll go get you a halter."

"I'll go with you," Bella said, darting off after him.

The horse Bella had been petting shook her head then turned her attention to Ava, staring at her as if expecting something.

"Don't look at me like that," she muttered. "I'm just the doctor."

Yeah. Keep telling yourself that, Ava.

The girl was a quick study when it came time to catching Little Red, the pony she would ride. All too soon they were headed back to the barn, Bella chatting the whole way about how she'd always wanted a horse, but her mom wouldn't let her have one until they were settled, but then they'd moved to Via Del Caballo and at last it's *finally* happening—all said in a rush and maybe without a breath between sentences. It made Carson smile.

"Mom, look," Bella called. "This is Little Red."

Ava was right where he'd left her, standing in the middle of the barn aisle, looking pensive.

"Last name—Riding Hood," Carson quipped.

And there it was again. The smile. The one that gave him pause and made him wonder how he could have ever thought his new doctor was average looking the first time he'd met her.

"Isn't she pretty, Mom?" Bella reached back and patted the mare's neck. "I love her."

"She is pretty, honey."

"Why don't you clip those ties right there to her halter?" Carson suggested, almost glad to turn away and help the little girl secure the horse between two rope ties. Ava stood back and watched.

She's a mom, he told himself. He'd never dated a mom before, and he wasn't about to start. And she was way smarter than he would ever be. A doctor. Successful. Top of her field. The complete opposite of him. He'd barely made it through college, had figured an education didn't matter when he'd be able to rope his whole life. Only now that might be taken away, and that made his stomach roll in the same sickening way it did on a boat.

"In the last room on the right, Bella—" he pointed down the barn aisle "—you'll find a box of brushes. Pick a few and I'll show you how to groom a horse."

Bella took off like a rabbit. She all but skipped down the aisle.

"She barely slept a wink all night."

He wasn't surprised. He'd seen her type before. Horse crazy to a T. Or maybe a capital H. "She seems like a good kid."

"The best."

Something about Ava's thoughtful expression had him studying her carefully. Her face unfolded into an expression of sorrow, but changed back so quickly he wondered if he'd imagined it.

"Listen. I was thinking maybe I could give her some lessons." He motioned with his chin toward his arm. "I'll be out of commission anyway, and it'd be a great way for me to earn some extra cash. Plus, it'll be easier to know what kind of horse she needs once she gets a little more experience."

"Lessons, wow." She crossed her arms in front of her, hugging herself tight. "She would love that."

"I wouldn't charge much. But if you'd rather not do business with a patient…"

"No, no. I'm fine with that."

"You don't have to decide right now. If you want to talk it over with your husband, and maybe Bella, too, you can get back to me."

He had no idea why he mentioned "husband," but the moment he did, he saw her flinch.

Her eyes swung away from his. "Bella's father passed away."

The words were so unexpected they rocked him back on his heels. "I'm sorry."

"It's okay. He died when she was two. I'm the only one that makes decisions in the family."

A widow. For at least six or seven years. So that meant she'd raised Bella on her own. Wow. What a remarkable woman.

"Great. Well, just let me know if you want to do it."

"Will these work?" Bella ran back down the aisle, slowing as she approached the horse, clearly worried she might frighten Little Red.

She learned quickly, he'd give her that.

"Those are perfect."

"Baby, I'm going to run some errands while you work with Mr. Gillian."

"Carson," he corrected.

"Aw, Mommy. Do you have to?"

"I'll be back in a flash." She came forward and hugged the little girl, kissing her on her head. "You'll have more fun without me."

"You don't have to leave," he said on her way by, worried he'd upset her.

"I know. I just have a really busy day."

He wanted to say something further. Words hovered on the tip of his tongue. But what to say? He'd already told her he was sorry.

"I'll see you later." She walked off without another word.

Chapter 3

She'd turned into a coward.

Why had she mentioned Paul? For the love of all that was holy, she'd almost told him that Bella wasn't her biological daughter, too. Whatever had possessed her? Usually she kept quiet about her personal life, and yet here she was opening up to him. She shouldn't have done that. She needed to keep things impersonal. She would be operating on him soon, for goodness' sake. That was all he was to her. A patient.

But later, when Bella came running out of the stable the moment she drove up, Ava knew she was kidding herself. She found the man ridiculously attractive. Years ago he'd have been just her type. She'd always been drawn to masculine, outdoorsy guys. She would not go down that road again.

"Mom, Carson needs to talk to you."

Oh, great. Just what she needed. "Okay, honey. I'm coming."

Bella took her hand, tugging her inside. She found Carson right where she'd left him, standing at one end of the barn, the horse he'd given to Bella to groom snorting in boredom, or so it sounded.

"Here she is."

If ever she needed evidence of how completely uninteresting Carson found her, she had it right then. He barely looked in her direction. She was just Dr. Moore to him. Nothing else. The realization deflated her shoulders.

"If she wants to ride, she'll need different shoes," he said.

"Can I ride? Can I? Huh?"

Bella's excitement was evident and Ava found herself glancing down at her daughter's feet. He must have read the confusion on her face.

"They have the wrong kind of heel," he said with a slight smile that made him even more handsome.

Oh, Ava. You have it so *bad.*

"Don't get me wrong," he added. "They're nice boots and all, but I bet you bought them at a department store, not a tack store."

She'd done exactly that. They sure looked like cowboy boots to her, though. "What's wrong with the heel?"

"It isn't tacked on right, not like real cowboy boots are. It'll come off if it bangs the stirrup hard enough. Plus the foot's too narrow. It'll slip through the stirrup and get her caught up if we're not careful. And they have that strap thing around the ankle, which means I can't put her in spurs. They might look like real cowboy boots, but they're not."

Well the store clerk sure hadn't made it sound that way. "So I need to go to a riding store."

"You're going to let me ride?" Bella squeaked.

"Not today." She took a deep breath. She'd given his offer some thought while she'd been out running errands. "Mr. Gillian has offered to give you some lessons, Bella. I think it's a good idea. That way we'll both know what we're getting into."

Bella stared up at her incredulously. Then, darting forward, she wrapped her hands around Ava's waist and hugged her as tightly as Ava had ever felt Bella hold her.

"Oh, Momma. Thank you so much."

Momma. She was in every sense of the word. Her throat tightened because she couldn't have loved Bella more than if she'd given birth to her herself. She inhaled, trying to keep the tears at bay. They'd been through so much together and yet here they were, starting a new life in a new town with a new hope for the future.

"You have to keep your grades up."

"I will." Bella leaned back, brown eyes so like Paul's and so filled with joy. "I promise."

Ava glanced up at Carson. He had the strangest expression on his face. Almost as if her daughter's reaction had moved him, too.

"Well, now that that's settled." She saw him take a deep breath. "You won't be able to find the boots you need at a department store. Try the local feed store. And while you're there, maybe get some boot-cut jeans, too."

She had no idea what those were, but she supposed she'd find out. "Where's the store?"

"If you hang on a moment, I can show you the place. I have to pick up some feed today anyway."

More time spent in the oh-too-distracting Mr. Carson Gillian's company. *Great.*

"Can we go today, Mom? Pleeezzz?" Bella's brown eyes were imploring. "Carson said I could ride tomorrow as long as I have the proper attire."

She knew she was fighting a losing battle. And, really, when else would she have time to do it? She should take advantage of a quiet cell phone while she could.

"Okay, sure."

"Cool!"

And that was how Ava found herself following Carson into downtown Via Del Caballo, a place that still felt unfamiliar to her. It'd been such a long road to get to where she was that she'd sworn to herself she'd get out more often. It seemed like she'd spent the last two months throwing herself into her job and taking care of Bella.

"Mmm. My hands smell so good." Bella held up a horse-stained palm for Ava's inspection. "Smell."

"No thank you." She wrinkled her nose. "I'll take your word for it."

"Do you think we might buy a horse from Carson?"

Ava glanced down, wishing like hell Paul could see her, all smiles and happiness. She'd been so gung ho to ride that horse. It reminded her so much of Paul. He'd been afraid of nothing, too.

"I think we'll have to wait and see."

"If we did, maybe I could keep it out at Gillian Ranch."

So she would have to deal with Carson on a regular basis? No thank you.

"Hmm. I don't think they board horses there."

"It sure is a nice ranch."

It was indeed. Ava couldn't imagine living among such splendor. She'd worked her butt off to get herself through medical school while raising Bella. The irony was that Bella had inherited a small fortune from her dad's insurance policy, but it was money she couldn't touch until she was much older. Paul had left Ava custody of Bella and nothing else, but that hadn't surprised her. They'd been about to get married when he'd fallen from the side of that mountain—an adrenaline junkie to the last. Foolish man.

The taillights of Carson's truck lit up and Ava forced herself to focus.

Via Del Caballo was a small town, one with numerous small ranches and farms that they'd passed on their way toward downtown. It was, as Ava liked to say, a one-stoplight town, although not literally. There was, however, a main drag—a street with a hairdresser, restaurant and, she suddenly realized, a feed store, not to mention cute little boutiques and other businesses. The walkways were all covered, potted plants hanging from between posts and the rafters. Quaint. That was what she called it, and why she'd decided to settle there.

She directed her SUV into a diagonal parking spot next to Carson's, the sound of his truck's diesel engine loud enough to temporarily drown out Bella's squeal when she spotted what looked like puppies in a wire kennel up against the front of the store.

Oh, dear goodness. The other thing Bella had always wanted.

"Mom. Look. Puppies." She grabbed the door handle.

Ava reached for her just in time. "Bella Marie Moore, don't you dare get out of this car." And this time her daughter actually listened. It must have been Ava's tone of voice because Bella glanced back at her with wide eyes. "We'll go in together."

Carson was waiting for her near the front of her SUV when they exited into bright summer sunshine. That was what she loved about Via Del Caballo. The weather. It cooled off at night thanks to an ocean on the other side of the coastal mountains, warming up once the overcast burned off. Beautiful weather. Gorgeous scenery thanks to the grass-covered hills and lush, ancient oaks. Cute little town with its single-lane street and stately homes near the center of downtown. She was renting one of those homes not far from where they stood.

"Ready to do some shopping?" he asked Bella.

Her daughter nodded, but Ava was clearly distracted. Carson's eyes followed her gaze, a smile coming to his face when he spotted the black-and-white puppies behind the wire cage.

"Uh-oh," he said.

She'd denied Bella a dog for years. Between finishing medical school, her residency and living in an apartment, she hadn't felt it feasible. But now they were settled and she knew in that instant she'd be going home with more than new boots today.

"Mom, can I pet them?"

Carson caught her gaze, his smile seeming to say, *You're in for it now.*

"It's not up to me, Bella. We'll have to ask the store owner."

"Oh, he won't mind." Carson's brows dropped when he smiled. On any other man those thick brows would be overpowering, but Carson had such a masculine face with a thick jaw and square chin that they suited him. "Come on. I'll introduce you."

Bella didn't want to leave the little pups behind, but Ava held out her hand, her meaning clear. Behind them a truck roared past, nearly drowning out what she said.

"Probably never going to get a dog."

Ava winced inside. The poor kid had been a trouper throughout the years. It hadn't been easy, just the two of them. Bella had gone without a lot most of the time. Once she'd completed her residency and been hired at Via Del Caballo General, Ava'd promised herself all that would change. No more scrimping. No more saving. Time to live a little. Time for Bella to enjoy the spoils of victory.

"Well, look who's here," said a man from behind a counter to the left of the doorway. His friendly eyes matched the gray in his hair, his black apron with VDC Farm & Feed printed on the front nearly wrapping all the way around his small frame. "The rodeo legend in the flesh."

"Hardly a legend," Carson said, holding up his elbow.

"Ouch. What happened there?"

"Broke my elbow. Surgery next week."

"Too bad."

"Tell me about it." Carson turned back to her. "Tom, this is Dr. Ava Moore and her daughter, Bella. They just moved here."

Tom's gray brows lifted above the rim of his glasses. "A doctor, huh? You don't look old enough to be one of those."

Maybe someday people would stop saying that, but she didn't take offense. It was hard not to instantly like that man with the wire glasses and graying hair.

"Nice to meet you, Tom." She smiled. "You have a nice store."

The place smelled like a shoe store and a waffle house, such a strange combination that she paused and took stock of her surroundings. Windows along the front allowed light to stream in. Stacks of bags of feed were piled to her left in multiple rows. That was where the sweetness came from, she realized. To her right stood a combination of clothing and horse equipment, bridles and saddles hanging along the long wall, the clothes in rounds to her right. Boots stood on a display in front of her, but Bella never gave them a glance.

"Are the puppies for sale?" Bella asked.

Above the rim of his glasses, Tom looked down at her daughter as he leaned across the counter, his weight on his elbows. "Well, now," said the older man, "that depends." He glanced past Bella and caught Ava's gaze. "You thinkin' you might want to buy one?"

Bella turned and glanced back. "Mom?"

It was decision time. Ava knew. And just as she'd known it was time to give Bella the first of her dreams—

riding lessons—she knew it was time to give her the second most sacred wish.

"Go ahead and look."

The way her daughter's face lit up, the way her whole
smile brightened, the excitement and happiness...well,
Ava suddenly wanted to cry again. This week would go
down in history, no doubt.

Bella was gone in an instant.

Carson met her gaze, brow raised. "A puppy and
horseback riding lessons all in one day," he said. "Kid's
living the dream."

She deserved it. Her kid should get a medal for all
she'd endured, not a puppy. Plus, maybe it would help
with the terrible dreams she'd been having lately.

"Ooh, Mom, look at that one."

She followed her daughter outside. Beneath the covered overhang, six adorable puppies had spotted Bella,
one of them balancing on its back paws, big brown eyes
staring up at her.

"Can I hold him?" Bella asked.

Tom had followed them outside. "Sure, sure. Let me
just undo the latch for you."

"Oh my goodness, what did you do to your thumb?"
Ava pointed to Tom's left hand and the tied-off white
gauze. She could see that blood had seeped through.

"I nicked it with a box cutter this morning."

"Let me see."

Tom looked at her sheepishly. "It's really nothing."

"Just the same."

The man glanced past Ava toward Carson, almost like
he was asking for backup, but Carson didn't say anything,
so he reluctantly gave her his thumb. Men. They were
always so reluctant to admit they were hurt.

She gently peeled the bandage down. "Looks like you might need a stitch or two."

"Nah. It'll heal up."

She gave the man his hand back. "Well, if it doesn't, call me. I'll stitch it for you. Free."

"Thanks." He turned back to the wire cage. It had four sides, a door seemingly concealed in the front of it. The moment that door was open the puppy burst into Bella's arms. Love at first sight, Ava thought. Mutual love. Bella started giggling and the puppy started to make a keening noise, not quite a whine but not exactly a bark, either.

"What kind of dogs are they?" Carson asked.

"Well now, there's the rub." Tom scratched his head with his good hand. "They're my neighbor's pups, actually. She works with border collies, but our other neighbor breeds Bernese mountain dogs, and damned if her stud didn't get out and somehow…well, you know. But they're cute as the dickens. That's why they have such big heads, though. It's actually a hybrid breed. Bordernese. They get that long coat from both parents, but they'll be good-size dogs. I hope you have a yard."

"We do," Bella said, then met her gaze. "Momma, can we please?"

"How much are they?" Not that it mattered.

"We're asking fifty dollars." Tom smiled. "A steal at twice the price."

Ava took a deep breath. "You can have one, Bella—"

Her daughter whooped in delight, the puppy thinking that meant it was play time, yipping in response. It wiggled in her arms, pink tongue trying to lick her face again.

"Bella," Ava said again, more loudly. "You need to promise me you'll take care of her. That you'll clean up after her and take her out to go potty and take her for walks every day."

"Actually that one's a boy," Tom said, pointing to the obvious boy parts.

"I'll take care of him." Bella stood, clutching the puppy to her. The little dog had moved on to trying to clean her daughter's face.

"Okay then. Put him down for now. We're here for riding boots and jeans, remember?"

"But what if someone buys him while we're inside?"

"That won't happen," Tom said, holding out his arms. "I'll put him behind the counter with me for safekeeping."

Bella, her beautiful brown eyes filled with so much happiness they seemed to glow, nodded. "You be good," she told the puppy. "I'll be right back."

Ava looked up in time to catch Carson's gaze. He was smiling at her in a way that made her think she might have surprised him in some way.

"You're going to need some puppy food," he said. "And some piddle pads." He surprised her then, using his good hand to touch her back. "But you're in luck. I'm an expert at puppy rearing. Come on. I'll help you out."

Chapter 4

For the first time in his life the fact that Carson had always been the one to take care of the ranch dogs came in handy. Of course, that'd changed in recent years. Life on the road meant he didn't have time to do that, but it felt good for some reason to show Ava and Bella around the store, advising them on what they'd need.

"Do you think I could get this collar, Mom?"

Carson turned and had to bite back a smile when he spotted the pink collar with the white daisies studded throughout.

"Not unless you want to humiliate the poor thing," Ava said. "Pick something a little more masculine."

"Actually leather is better for them. It doesn't chafe like the nylon."

Bella nodded and headed back to the display. They'd already picked out a pair of boots for her and some jeans. She'd rushed through the whole process, though, wanting to get back to her puppy.

"I hope your backyard is puppy-proof."

"I think so," Ava said. "I hope so."

Carson echoed her words with his eyes. *Think?*

She'd clearly understood his silent question. "Well, I mean, I have no idea if there's ever been a dog back there. I didn't ask the landlord."

He nodded. "Well then, I suppose we're going to have to go look."

Ava frowned. "Don't you have feed to pick up or something? I'd hate for us to waste half your day."

He did, but he felt a ridiculous need to impress her. Ridiculous because he suspected he knew the reason why. He'd come across her type before. The cutting horse industry drew people with money. Once upon a time he'd let himself fall for one of his dad's clients. Katarina had been rich and beautiful, a lawyer from the Bay Area, and he'd been sure she was "the one." Right up until the day he'd overheard her best friend mimicking his drawl— only he didn't drawl—and Katarina had laughed and said something about brains being overrated. The words still stung. Just because he wasn't college educated didn't mean he was dumb.

But that was why he heard himself say, "They're probably already loading the feed." Still trying to prove himself, he supposed.

"Already done," the older man said. "Full pallet of Stable Mix in the bed of your truck."

He turned back to Ava. She didn't seem like she approved of the idea, and that sort of hurt.

"Can he come over, Momma, please? I don't want Balto to get out of our backyard."

"Balto…like the movie?" her mom asked.

She nodded.

Ava just smiled. "I'm pretty sure I can dog-proof our yard. Or hire someone to do it."

"But can you tell which plants might be poisonous to canines?"

Ava's brows shot up. "No."

Just as he'd thought. See, there really were some things you couldn't learn in books. "Then you should probably let me have a look around."

"Please?" Bella asked.

"Okay, fine." She must have realized her words had come out sounding harsh because she said, "We would appreciate your help very much. Thank you."

Not really. He could tell she wanted to keep him at arm's length. He didn't know if that was because of client/patient privacy or something else, but he supposed it didn't matter. He felt the same way, too. He just wanted her to think of him as more than a slab of meat when she operated on him. And, if he were honest with himself, being with her and her kid distracted him from thinking about his upcoming surgery.

As it turned out, they didn't have all that far to go. She lived in the older part of town. The "fancy side," he liked to call it. An area with stately Victorian homes, most built before the turn of the century when the area had been a booming cattle town. Her house was dark gray with white and maroon trim, and had likely been owned by one of the town's founders back in the day. It would have been L-shaped if not for the rectangular section that sprouted from the crook of the L, one capped by a witch's-hat turret with dormer windows all around it. Gable roofs capped both ends of the L, square windows set into the corners. A porch framed the middle section, the white balcony railings matching a similar porch on the second floor.

"Nice," he muttered to himself. How many times had he dreamed of building a similar place on his family's property? One day he hoped to do exactly that, but for now he slid out of his truck, curious about the inside.

"Isn't it neat?" Bella said as she came around the side of the house where Ava must have parked, her new puppy wiggling in her arms. "My mom said it's like something out of a Norman Rockwell painting, whoever that was."

"It's great," he admitted to Bella.

"Come on." She giggled when Balto tried to jump down.

Ava came around the corner right as he reached the pathway leading to her porch. "Short drive, huh?" she asked, green eyes bright.

"Short commute for you, too."

"It is," she admitted, unlocking the front door.

"I've always wanted to build a place like this on my father's ranch."

She held up a hand for a moment, her gaze following her daughter. "Bella, if you put that puppy on the ground, you better watch him."

"I will, Mom."

Carson followed Ava into the foyer and stopped. She did, too, turning back to him with a curious expression on her face. "It's funny you should say that," she said. "I always thought this place might have been one of the original ranch homes back in the day. It's so big. I could picture it surrounded by pastures and horses and cattle."

He could, too. "I bet these floors are original." He tapped the hardwood with his toe. It was a burnished gold thanks to the sunlight pouring in from the frosted glass in the front door.

"Wait until you see my favorite part." She turned to their right and the sitting area that ran along the front of the house. He knew immediately what she would point to because he'd admired it a million times, too, but from the street. Set into the tops of divided-light windows was stained glass, each section different. One panel was all roses. One was tulips. One had colorful daisy-type flowers. They turned the floor of the family room into a kaleidoscope of color.

"I've seen that before in older homes," he told her. "I think it's a turn-of-the-century thing."

"It's what sold me on the house."

"Did you buy it?" She'd mentioned a landlord earlier and so he didn't think so.

"No. But I asked for a lease with an option. I wasn't sure if I should live in the city or out in the country just yet."

He wouldn't exactly call Via Del Caballo a city. It was too small for that. More like a town.

"I'm guessing Bella's voting for the country."

"You betcha." She smiled ruefully. "A place where she can have chickens and goats and horses."

"Not goats. Goats smell."

"They do?"

"Well, the male ones do."

"Speaking of that, maybe we should check out the backyard so we don't have a smelly problem in here."

Motioning for her to lead the way, Carson admired the vaulted ceilings and the craftsmanship of the house. Chair rails with panels beneath, crown molding, the hand-carved balustrade that stretched along the heavy oak steps that led to a second story.

"Man, this place is really something."

"Do you like old homes?" They'd passed through a kitchen with fixtures that looked old-fashioned but that he would bet just seemed that way. She'd paused with her back against a door that probably led to the outside. Bella was off somewhere with her new puppy.

"Don't tell anyone, but I secretly wanted to be an architect."

"Really?"

He nodded. "Success in an arena always came easy for me, so easy, I'd get bored from time to time. So I build furniture to keep myself busy."

That seemed to shock her even more, and it sort of

solidified his belief that she thought of him as nothing more than a cowboy. "What kind of furniture?"

"All kinds. Tables, chairs, beds."

Something flickered in her eyes and whatever it was had him straightening and paying closer attention. It was the same damn sensation he'd had back at the ranch, a sort of out-of-body experience that made him see things differently. The light from the windows in the door back-lit her hair and highlighted the unusual green of her eyes.

"A man of hidden talents," she said.

Her voice had lowered, gotten softer, and he realized then what it was about her that had him so on edge.

He *liked* her. She was nothing like Katarina or her friends. There was a warmth to her, an air of caring that shone from her eyes and that she bestowed on the people around her. Even the feed store owner, Tom. She'd offered to fix his finger. For free.

"I'm pretty good with horses, too."

The tension in the air seemed to thicken like a summer thunderstorm.

"I hope so." She thrust open the door, almost as if she felt the heat in the air, too. "For Bella's sake."

And maybe she did.

He's a patient. *A patient.*

The cool air hit Ava's face with fingers that made her shiver. She all but bolted from him as she stepped down the stairs that led to her backyard.

A patient.

This was why one should never get personally involved with someone they were treating. How many times had her professors warned of that very thing? It was okay to care, just not too much. You needed to remain objective. Noticing how well he filled out his white T-shirt was not remaining objective.

"It looks like something out of a Disney movie."

She forced herself to focus and admitted that it did. Flowers framed the yard. Red ones, pink ones, white ones… all different colors and kinds. She liked to think it'd been done on purpose, to match the stained glass in the family room. When she'd looked at the home before renting it, she'd had the sensation that it'd been loved by the women who'd lived there throughout the centuries.

"But you realize your puppy's going to tear those flower beds apart."

"You think?"

"Oh, yeah. And kill your lawn. Well, not all of it, but some. Is your landlord okay with that?"

She shrugged. "He said we could have a pet."

He turned, headed to the side of the house. "If I was you, I'd put a kennel out here, on the side. You can leave Balto in there when you're gone."

"Good idea."

He turned to face her. "Bella's going to have to learn to be responsible. She'll have to take Balto on walks and clean up after him. It's a bit like owning a horse."

"It'll be good for her." She faced the back of the house, looking up. Carson wondered if she was staring at Bella's room. "It's been tough for her."

"The move?" he asked.

"That and other things."

He was quiet for a moment, his hand lifting to stroke his chin, and she wondered if his razor stubble was soft or sharp.

Ava!

"You know, horses are great therapy animals."

"So I've heard."

"I think you're doing the right thing by getting her involved with them."

Was she? Sometimes she wondered if she did anything right where Bella was concerned. What nobody told you when you had a kid was how hard it was. How there were times when all you wanted to do was cover your head with a pillow and scream because, as they got older, kids developed a mind of their own and sometimes that mind didn't want to cooperate. And then there were those moments when she wouldn't change anything for the world. Those were the times when she most missed Paul. He would have loved seeing her today.

"Thank you. For everything."

"You can repay me by fixing my arm." He lifted the limb in question, pointing. "I didn't realize until you told me how bad it was just how much roping means to me."

As if she needed a reminder of the importance of his surgery. But she did need one, she supposed. He was her patient. She'd be operating on him. Best not to get too close.

"Don't forget to let me know how much you want to be paid."

"I'll leave that up to you."

"Mo-om!"

A face appeared at the window Ava had been staring at earlier. "Balto had an accident."

Ava shook her head ruefully. "And so it begins."

"I should get going anyway."

She nodded. "See you tomorrow for lessons."

He let himself out the side entrance to the yard. Ava watched him go, thinking the nurses would go nuts when they saw him Monday. Daring cowboys who chased gold buckles were the stuff of romantic dreams. Not hers, though. She was too rooted in reality. Dealing with life and death had a way of grounding a person. What she needed was a man who'd be there for her. Someone she could talk to after a long day at work. Who'd put her needs, if not first, pretty close to it.

Men who chased world championships weren't on her list.

Chapter 5

He hoped this didn't end up being the biggest mistake of his life.

"Do I get to saddle my own horse today?"

Bella tugged on Little Red's lead line, as if she hoped to make the horse walk faster back to the barn. Maybe she *was* hoping to do that.

"You do." Carson lifted his hat, smoothing back his hair. The day had dawned bright and unseasonably warm. Perfect riding weather, although he suddenly dreaded helping the little girl. The fact was he'd never given riding lessons before. Oh, sure, he'd helped out his brothers and sister when he'd been growing up. They'd all razzed each other over the years. But there was a big difference between teasing your siblings and actually teaching a little girl how to ride.

With her mother watching.

They rounded the corner of the barn, Ava's body silhouetted by sunlight. She seemed immersed in staring at her phone, although she did look up when they entered, a smile coming to her face.

"Go ahead and put her on the cross ties like I taught you."

The kid was a quick study. He'd give her that. Probably got her smarts from her mom. She had Little Red anchored in no time flat.

"Are you wearing your new boots?" he asked Bella.

"I am." She stopped and lifted her pant leg.

"Awesome. Let's go get some brushes and the saddle."

His hands shook, he realized, tucking them into his jeans, or trying to. He couldn't do much with his right arm. It must be the whole lesson thing. He glanced over at Ava again. Still had her nose in the phone, her face in profile as she leaned against the stable wall, her hair pulled back in a ponytail. It made her look even younger than her years.

Pretty.

So, all right. Okay. He found her attractive. Big deal. He doubted she gave him a second thought once she was away from the ranch.

"Will I get to gallop today?"

Carson slipped the saddle over his good arm. "Hold on there, *pardner.* You won't be doing much more than a trot on Little Red today."

Bella's face fell. "But what if I do really well?"

"Grab those brushes." He managed to hook a bridle over his bad arm. "First you learn to walk, then you can run," he said sternly.

He set the saddle on the ground near where Little Red was tied as Bella went to work grooming.

Mom was still on her phone.

Why did he keep glancing over at her? He was like some teen in school unable to stop peeking glances at the pretty girl.

"Mom. You should come pet Little Red."

"That's okay," Ava said distractedly.

"My mom doesn't like horses."

What? His gaze swung back to Ava just in time to see her head pop up. "That can't be true," he said.

"It is." Bella's words were matter-of-fact. "She says

it's hard to support a hobby when you don't trust the athletic equipment."

"Bella!"

"It's true, Mom."

The cool and composed Dr. Moore didn't like horses. Interesting.

"I don't dislike them." She tucked her phone in her back pocket. "I just don't…like their big teeth."

She made him want to smile. He had a feeling there wasn't much Dr. Ava Moore was afraid of. The fact that what scared her was one of the sweetest and most trusting animals on God's green earth amused him.

"Come on over."

"That's okay."

"Mo-om."

He saw her take a deep breath. Saw her shoot her daughter a death glare. But damn if she didn't push away from the wall.

"It won't bite, will it?"

He smiled. "Not unless I tell her to."

Bella giggled. Ava eyed the horse askance.

"He's kidding, Mom. Horses don't bite."

"Well, actually, some do, but not Red. Seriously. It's okay."

His words seemed to do little to reassure her. She had the same look on her face as someone about to approach a tiger with a chair. Her fear made his stomach do something funny, although what it was, he couldn't name.

He reached for her hand. Her eyes shot to his. He tried to ignore how pretty they looked this morning with sunlight illuminating their depths.

"Just hold your palm flat."

She resisted at first. The horse's ears pricked forward just before it reached to sniff her open palm and, when it did, she glanced back at him. And there it was again, that magical grin, the one that turned his insides out.

"See," Carson said, moving in closer even though he told himself not to. "They're not all bad."

"Its nose is so soft."

She smelled like spring.

He let her go, stepped back and turned to Bella. "Ready to learn how to saddle a horse?"

"Heck yeah." Bella bounced up on her toes.

Carson chastised himself the whole time he helped Bella get mounted up. There was getting to know your doctor and then there was getting personal. Touching Ava had been personal. With his surgery this week, he should focus on the first, not the second.

"Ready to ride?" he asked Bella. When he glanced back at Ava it was in time to see her frown.

"Relax, Doc. She'll be fine."

Her expression clearly said, "Famous last words."

He smiled, leading Red to the arena out back. A light breeze bent the tips of the blades of grass that framed the pathway.

"All right. Let's put you up."

Bella was like a puppy about to be fed. She practically danced toward him. He moved up alongside Red, motioning Bella over.

Ava stood outside the arena and part of him wished she'd disappear like she had yesterday. But he supposed he didn't blame her for sticking around. It made him even more nervous, though.

"Okay, so here's what you're going to do." He moved into position to demonstrate. "You're going to put your left foot in the stirrup like this." Fortunately Little Red lived up to her name. She was on the shorter side, so it was no worse than putting his foot on the top rung of a step stool. "Then you grab the horn and pull yourself up. Like this." Red stood patiently while he swung a leg over.

"I want to try."

"Okay." He hopped off. "Just put your foot right there."

It was like the kid had been doing it her whole life. She was fearless as she climbed aboard.

"Wow. That was great."

Bella swung around in the saddle. "Look, Mom. I'm riding." And her smile was so full of delight it was hard not to grin back.

"Good job, honey," Ava called.

He wondered how hard it was for Ava to sound so enthusiastic. He would have to give her credit. Here she was allowing her daughter to do something she herself was afraid to do.

"Let's walk, okay?"

Bella's nod was so enthusiastic it had to make her dizzy. He kept a hand on Bella's calf above the stirrup and one on Red as the horse began to move. So far, so good.

"Oh, wow." Bella's voice was full of awe, and the look on her face? It was so full of delighted happiness that his heart did that weird thing again, only this time for a whole different reason. He forgot sometimes what it was like for first-timers to ride.

"Okay, so to steer, you just move the reins in the direction you want to go. Right to turn right. Left to go left. Simple. Go ahead and try it."

She jerked the reins toward her mom. Red lifted her head in protest.

"Gently. You can't go pulling on their mouths like that. They don't like it."

Bella's whole face crumbled. "I'm sorry, Red."

Adorable. He almost forgot about her mom watching them with an eagle eye.

"Go ahead and try it again."

Bella thrust her tongue up against her teeth. She gave the reins a feather-light pull. Red obediently turned for her.

"I did it."

"You did. Now try it all by yourself."

"Oh, no." Ava's words were just a tick away from sounding panicked. "I don't think she's ready for that."

"Mo-om. I'm fine."

And she was. He let go and Red took great care of her, so much so that Carson found himself moving to the rail, leaning against it to watch. Maybe he wasn't such a bad teacher after all.

"Turn the other way," he called out.

Bella's smile was as radiant as the heavens.

"This is a dream come true for her."

He'd been hoping to impress Ava for some silly reason and he knew in that instant that he'd succeeded. It should have filled him with relief, but that wasn't what he felt as he stared at her. There was such a look of sadness mixed with joy that he couldn't take his gaze away.

He'd thought about her last night, about how driven she must have been to succeed, about how women like that were usually high-maintenance. But as he looked into her eyes he realized she hadn't worked hard for herself; she'd done it for Bella.

"It's been tough on her—my schooling, her dad dying, me being gone for hours on end during my residency. Some days I worry she'll be in therapy for the rest of her life because of everything she's been through."

He had to look away, watch as Bella walked her pony around the arena.

Her dad dying. It was the second time she'd said it that way.

"How long were you married?"

Ava looked down, rubbed at a spot on her hand. "We weren't, actually. Bella's not mine. Well, she's mine in every sense of the word that matters. Heart and soul. Her mom died right after she was born. I met Paul when Bella was one year old."

She glanced at him quickly before her eyes drifted over to Bella. "It was one of those things that just sort of happens. We fell in love hard and fast. And then... he was gone and Bella was left with no one but me. So I adopted her. We both don't have any family, so it was either that or foster care, and I wasn't about to let that happen. Fortunately he'd already named me guardian if anything happened to him, which it did." And then in a voice so low he almost didn't hear her, and probably wouldn't have if not for the breeze that kicked her words right to his ears, she said, "Stupid man."

She looked sad again and he'd have to have been an unfeeling son of a gun not to ache on her behalf. Sure, he'd thought about how hard it must have been on her personally and financially, but he hadn't given a thought to the emotional toll it'd taken on her. He might not be a father but that didn't mean he didn't understand how difficult it must have been for her to walk out that door every day, leave Bella with strangers, to have to split her time between being a good mom and being a good student.

"You amaze me."

She glanced at him sharply.

He reeled himself back, having started to sink into the grief in her eyes, and he couldn't allow himself to do that. Doctor. Mother. Grieving widow. So many reasons to steer clear.

"Must be tough on her to be without a father."

She considered his words before saying, "She doesn't know any different."

"Probably not." He watched the waves of sadness for a moment. "I guess in some ways that's lucky. I still miss my mom every day of my life."

"And I miss Paul."

Thoughts of his mom made his stomach churn, too. "Well. This is a cheerful conversation, isn't it?"

"I'm about ready to prescribe us both antidepressants."

"Nah." He waved toward Bella. "All you need to do is look at the smile on that girl's face."

She met his gaze and he saw something he didn't expect. Hope. It was only then that he realized how deeply she buried the pain of Paul's passing.

"Thank you."

He pushed away from the rail, feeling the need to move again, to turn away from her, to remind himself that he was there to do a job.

"Let's see if she's up to a trot."

"Oh, no. Do you have to?"

"I've got this."

Her eyes were the same color as the grass behind her. "I know you do."

Chapter 6

It had been a magical day, Ava thought as she slipped into bed that night. Special and wonderful and totally unexpected.

"Momma?"

Ava sat up in bed, switching on the light on her nightstand. Bella's tear-stained cheeks glistened.

"Honey, what is it?" She almost got out of bed, but Bella ran over to her, all but throwing herself into her arms. "Was it the nightmare again?"

She felt rather than saw Bella nod. She nestled her chin into her hair, pulling her close. Damn it. She'd been hoping the realization of one of her dreams—horses—might give her sweet dreams. Then again, it seemed like any time Bella was overexhausted, one of the bad dreams occurred, and today had been tiring for them all.

"I don't want to go back to my own bed."

"Did you want to go get Balto?"

They'd decided to keep the puppy in the new kennel she's spent a small fortune to have delivered and erected that morning. Fewer accidents that way.

"No," Bella said. "I want to stay here."

"Okay," Ava said, leaning back so they could lie side by side, Bella's teary gaze staring out at her. "You can sleep here tonight." The little girl blinked and the sadness in her eyes broke Ava's heart.

Bella had been so young when Paul had died, too

young to remember much. She'd been told he died in an accident, but that was all she'd know until she was older, and then she'd be told the truth about the tragic climbing mishap that had taken Paul's life.

Bella's mind had filled in the blanks, probably thanks to all of Paul's adventure photos she used to have around their old place, but those she hadn't had the heart to put up when they'd moved. She'd hoped that might help, too. So far nothing had kept the bad dreams at bay, not even a therapist, and a part of Ava still worried that she'd failed Bella somehow.

"What was it this time?"

"Same," Bella said, already seeming to get sleepy. "He was about to fall and I was trying to stop it from happening."

The funny thing was, Bella had never been told the details of Paul's death. A hiking accident, that's all she knew. He'd taken a tumble and hit his head. Ava became more and more convinced that something in her two-year-old mind had understood what happened. Or maybe she'd overheard something. Ava didn't know. She just hated the effect it had on her.

"Go to sleep now." She pulled her closer. "I've got you. Nobody's going anywhere."

It was a familiar litany that lulled Ava to sleep, too, but when she woke in the morning her mood wasn't as bright as it normally was. It was a school day, and a work day for her, which meant rushing around the house getting things ready for Bella and then for later that night when she'd have to come home and cook. Provided all went well at the hospital. That had her thinking of something else. Carson. Today was his pre-op. Tomorrow she'd operate on him. Another thing that stressed her out, which was super ridiculous because his surgery would be a piece of cake.

The tension in her neck didn't abate with the passing of the morning. Not even a particularly challenging microfracture she had to repair on a kid who'd fallen off a skateboard had helped her to focus. She loved helping kids. She just wished she knew how to make her own feel better.

"Your pre-op is in room 303."

Ava took a deep breath. "Thank you." Still, her hand rested on the door handle a moment before pushing into the room.

And there he sat, the man who'd put a smile on her daughter's face. Who'd lifted her kid's spirits in ways they hadn't been lifted in years. The man who couldn't wait to get back on a horse and ride off into the sunset.

"You look like someone who lost their best friend."

She had to take another deep breath before she could look him in the eyes. Yesterday, outside the arena, she'd felt something, a something that had scared her to death.

"Been a long day." She pasted a smile on her face and, as silly as it seemed, she felt ridiculously grateful that she'd dressed the part of a doctor today: tan slacks, white lab coat, hair pulled back in a ponytail. Sure, it was her normal uniform. So what if she'd brushed on some lip gloss a few minutes ago?

"You should try living on a ranch. Sunup to sundown."

"I'm sure."

His smile was so much like Paul's—part best friend, part natural-born flirt—that for a moment she couldn't breathe. What was it with men like him? They sauntered around as if a meteorite could land on their head and not hurt them.

"It's kind of strange for me to be sitting around so much."

"Yeah, well, after you have surgery, *no* riding."

"For how long?"

"Six weeks at best. Longer if you don't heal as quickly as others."

He didn't take the news well. But then she saw his chest expand, and if she wasn't mistaken, he might have nodded. "Okay, so what's on the agenda today?"

"We want to make sure you're healthy enough for surgery, so we'll be drawing some blood, checking your heart, that kind of thing." She opened his chart on her tablet and it felt good to put her doctor hat on. "I see you've already had your BP and temperature taken, and that looks good." She swiped to another page. "And the health questionnaire Laura gave you looks good. My anesthesiologist will want to talk to you before you leave, too. Surgery still looks good for tomorrow morning." She closed his chart. "What?"

He put a brave smile on when he said, "Nothing," but she knew better.

"Worried about surgery?"

He shook his head. But she wasn't fooled. That was, indeed, his concern. She could see it in his eyes.

"Carson, this is about as routine a surgery as you can get. Plus, I'm a good surgeon. I even had one of the highest scores when I sat for my boards. You won't find another surgeon as well qualified as I am."

"It's not really about the surgery."

His words gave her such a sense of relief that she took stock of the reason why. She'd been afraid he might be one of those male chauvinists, the kind that might secretly want an older, *male* doctor to do his operation. No denying what a relief it was to realize that wasn't the case.

"It's that my mom died while she was under general anesthesia, and I suppose it brings back old memories."

She caught a glimpse of rueful embarrassment before he dropped his gaze. She watched as he took a deep breath before squaring his shoulders and meeting her gaze again.

"I know it's ridiculous. My mom was sick and I'm not, but I guess deep down inside I'm a little afraid."

Afraid he wouldn't wake up. She'd heard it a thousand times.

"It's very safe. We eliminate much of the risk beforehand. That's why we have you meet with the anesthesiologist. You'll see. It'll be easy."

"I'm sure it will."

Before she could think better of it, she reached for his hand…and immediately wished she hadn't. It took her less than half a second to realize her touch was a little too personal. While she prided herself on her bedside manner, she tried not to cross the line.

Who was she kidding? She'd crossed the line where he was concerned days ago.

But then he pulled his hand away and, instead of feeling relief, she sensed something close to disappointment. Crazy.

"I'll be fine," he said with an air of bravado she knew was false. "Just nerves."

She had a feeling it wasn't easy for him to admit how deeply the thought of surgery affected him. That would be so typical of this type of man. They bulldozed their way through life until something reached out and slapped them down.

"We have things we can do to help you with that—your fear, I mean. Lots of people are afraid before surgery. I'll prescribe you something."

He looked up and met her gaze. "Thanks."

"I promise you. Everything will be fine."

He stared so deeply into her eyes that it felt like he touched her soul. It made her want to pull away from him.

"I'm going to hold you to that," he said.

She'd never been such a nervous wreck. See. That was the problem with getting involved with your patients. You lost your objectivity.

"He sure is a handsome hunk of man," said her scrub nurse as she walked into the operating room on Tuesday, her eyes above the blue mask full of amused interest. Ava just shook her head. She'd known this would happen.

His cast had been removed earlier, an ink stain marking the spot where she'd cut into his arm. She'd put a brace on his arm post-op, the kind that always reminded her of blood pressure cuffs thanks to the way it wrapped around a patient's upper arm and lower arm, leaving the elbow section bare, save for the brace that connected all four pieces. They would need to keep it exposed so they could check his incisions.

"You think he works out?"

Okay. That did it. "He's a patient, Nurse Bell, not a sex object."

One of the other OR nurses, someone whose name she didn't know, peered up at her from above her mask, her eyes wide. Dr. Hanover, her anesthesiologist, also looked up sharply.

Nurse Bell's eyes had dimmed. "Yes, ma'am."

And now look what she'd done. She didn't want to be "that" doctor, the one the nurses hated to work for. She was too new to the job to be stepping on toes, no matter how right she was to point out that ogling a patient was unprofessional.

"Are we ready, Dr. Hanover?" Ava asked a few minutes later, Carson's face covered with a laryngeal mask.

"We're good to go," said the older man, watching his monitors closely.

She lost herself in the delicate surgery then. It wasn't a particularly difficult one. She'd have a much tougher one later this afternoon—a proximal femoral shaft fracture—but that didn't mean she wasn't just as tense and just as on edge. She knew Carson. Appreciated what he was doing for Bella, so perhaps that was why she spent more time than usual repairing his damaged bone.

"Okay. I think we're good," she said less than an hour later. "Dr. Hanover, you can stop the anesthesia."

She checked the Velcro straps on his black splint, making sure it was secure enough. He'd have it on for at least a few weeks, probably more. With any luck he'd be back to riding horses in a couple months. But all in all, she was pleased with how things went. They wheeled Carson out, Ava stripping her gloves off. She'd check on him later.

But when she ducked into the recovery room after she'd washed up, he was still out cold. Sometimes that happened.

"He's taking his sweet time opening his eyes," the recovery room nurse said.

"Are his vitals okay?"

"They're fine." The nurse's eyes twinkled. "Just as fine as he is."

Ava bit back a retort. She'd already chastised one nurse today. She moved in a little closer.

"Carson," she said. "You can wake up now."

It was as if he'd been waiting for her. His eyes snapped open. She felt herself relax because, despite what she'd told Carson, there was always the fear that a patient wouldn't wake up. Usually she didn't think about such things, but today she had, and he'd clearly be just fine. He even tried to move. The surgery straps held him down.

The nurse stationed herself on his other side. "Mr. Gillian. I'm Nurse Diaz. I'll be with you while you wake up. Are you cold? Do you need a blanket?"

"Who?"

"Nurse Diaz."

"Where's she?"

"Where's who?" Nurse Diaz asked.

"Good-lookin' doctor."

Nurse Diaz snorted, pinning Ava with a stare that held amusement and maybe even a touch of envy. Ava shook her head. Patients said the damnedest things when they were coming out of anesthesia.

"She's right there." Nurse Diaz nodded in her direction.

Carson tried to sit up again.

"Whoa. Don't do that." The nurse placed a hand on his chest even though Carson couldn't sit up. "Just relax."

Carson's eyes went big just before he smiled. "There she is."

Ava tried not to laugh at the look on Carson's face. It was as if he'd spotted his most favorite toy in the whole, wide world.

"S'pretty," he said on his way back down.

Nurse Diaz laughed. Ava meant to shoot her a look of reprimand, but she would bet it wouldn't come off as very authoritarian, not with the smile she tried so hard to keep off her face. Despite the fact that she knew there could never be a future with him, his words filled her with a burst of purely feminine delight.

He thought she was pretty. How nice.

"Keep an eye on him," Ava said. "He's a personal friend."

The woman lifted a brow and Ava quickly clarified. "He's teaching my daughter how to ride."

"Ride?" Carson tried sitting up again. "What horse'll we ride?"

Once a cowboy, always a cowboy, she thought, turning away.

"Wait," Carson called.

The nurse encouraged him to lie down. Carson turned his head, searching for her.

"Ava, go ride with me."

The recovery room nurse clearly fought off laughter. Ava felt heat stain her cheeks red.

"He's confusing me with my daughter." Ava felt the need to explain.

"Surrrre," drawled Nurse Diaz.

"He is," Ava said. But it was clear Diaz was teasing her, and that was better than being afraid of her, she supposed, so she let the matter drop.

"Wait." Carson tried to sit up again. She was almost to the door and she had no idea how he managed to undo the OR straps without the use of his right arm, but he managed to lift his shoulders enough to make eye contact again. She stopped with her hand on the door.

"I wanna date." He fell back to the bed. "Take on a date."

The way the nurse's shoulders shook, and her eyes glittered, put Ava on the defense. "It's just the anesthesia talking." Goodness, her cheeks were probably as red as the emergency sign outside the ER.

The nurse cocked up another brow. "Best truth serum around."

She ducked her head. The nurse chuckled softly as Ava got out of there before she lost complete control of her emotions.

He liked her. He thought she was pretty. Wanted to take her on a date. It shouldn't matter, but for some reason it did. Maybe she hadn't been sucked dry by her career and motherhood. It was just too bad she'd never date a man like him...no matter how tempting.

Chapter 7

What the heck had they given him?

Carson tried to keep his eyes open but couldn't seem to do it, the room they'd parked him in so bright he had to squint against the light. His elbow hurt. And he had a splint on his arm now.

But he hadn't died.

Even in his foggy state of mind the thought registered with such astounding clarity that he smiled. A nurse filled his vision.

"Do you need anything, Mr. Gillian?"

Ava. He wanted Ava.

He opened his mouth, tried to form words. "Thank. You."

"You're welcome, Mr. Gillian."

No. He wanted to thank Ava. He wanted to tell her what a great doctor she was. And that he appreciated her hard work. And that he liked her.

His elbow throbbed.

Or he'd like to like her…except he couldn't. Why couldn't he like her? He couldn't remember his reasons.

"Do you need something for pain?"

As much as he wanted it, he shook his head then immediately wished he hadn't. Nausea overwhelmed him. He closed his eyes.

How long he was out, he had no idea. When he woke up next, Ava stared down at him, a professional smile on her face, hair pulled back, white doctor's coat matching the sheets on his hospital bed. He sat in a room with a curtain partition on either side of him, nurses moving back and forth.

"Hello," she said.

His head throbbed in time with his arm. "'Lo."

"How are you feeling now?"

"Pain," he said, looking down at his arm. At least this time the room didn't spin.

"That will pass." She glanced at her tablet, almost as if she didn't want to look him in the eyes, but before her lashes swooped down he caught a glimpse of something that seemed like embarrassment. "You took a while to wake up. Do remember us talking earlier?"

Talking? When? He shook his head.

She looked…relieved? "That happens sometimes. Don't worry." Her eyes scanned his face and then his elbow. Satisfied with what she saw, she straightened. "We're getting ready to send you down for an X-ray. We want to make sure everything's in place. Afterward, we'll fit you with a special splint and, if you're feeling up to it, you can go home. I've spoken with your family and they'd like to come see you while we wait for someone from radiology to come get you. Would that be okay?"

"'Course."

Ava turned as if about to leave, but he called her back. "Hey."

She swung to face him and he was certain of it now. She was having a hard time looking him in the eye.

"Thanks."

She nodded. "My pleasure." She tried to turn away again.

"Don't you want to stick around for my family?" A nurse had come forward to help him sit up, smiling. Any other time he would have smiled back, but today he had eyes only for Ava. "I'm sure they'd like to shake your hand, too."

"That's okay." She clutched her tablet to her chest. "I've already spoken to them."

"Yes, but you haven't formally met any of them."

"Well, no, but…"

"Stay."

Ava glanced at the nurse, who hadn't moved away. He did, too. The younger woman stared down at him with a bemused smile on her face and it triggered a memory. Something he'd said earlier. Something he couldn't quite remember but had a feeling he probably should.

"I have other patients—"

"There he is!" someone called.

Shane, home for the week, his eyes bright and teasing as he rounded the corner of the curtain. His dad, Reese, was in his wake, followed by Maverick and his aunt and uncle. Heck, his whole damn family had come to see him, all but Jayden who still stubbornly refused to speak to their dad. She'd call him later, she'd said.

"What are you guys doing here?" Carson asked. "Maverick said he had this handled."

"You didn't think we'd trust Maverick to do this on his own, did you?" asked Shane, his black cowboy hat nearly the same shade as his thick brows.

"Hey, now," said Maverick, who was younger by a couple of years but shared their eyes. All the Gillians had dark hair and blue eyes, although Maverick was the better looking of all the brothers, so he'd been told. The most serious, too, which was why Carson had asked him to take him home from the hospital.

"You feeling okay, son?" Reese Gillian looked a little worried. His dad took Carson's rodeo career seriously. Probably more seriously than Carson did lately. Once his mom had died, it'd taken the wind out of Carson's sails.

His priorities had changed and success had seemed… well, unnecessary in a way. Which was why his reaction to his injury had surprised him. Knowing he might never rope again had scared the hell out of him. Made him want to try harder to get back into the arena.

"Doc says your elbow's going to be fine."

"Hurts a little," he said to the room at large.

"We'll give you some instruction on how to ice it when you go home," Ava said.

His aunt broke away from the crowd. "Hi," she said to Ava, sweeping her long grey hair over her shoulder. "We didn't get to meet earlier. I'm Carson's aunt Crystal."

Ava took Crystal's hand. "Nice to meet you."

Both women glanced at him, Crystal's eyes filled with laughter. "I hear Carson here gave you a tough time in the recovery room."

Ava seemed confused. Carson knew how she felt.

"What do you mean?" Ava asked.

"After surgery. My friend's daughter works here. Maggie Bell. Her mom and I were in high school together. She said a couple of the other nurses heard my nephew talking to you in the recovery room."

Ava's brows shot up. "Nurse Bell heard about that?"

Crystal's blue eyes sparkled. "I guess all the nurses are talking about it."

"What?" He glanced around the room and could tell by the looks on everyone's faces that they all knew it, too. Whatever "it" was, it amused them. Everyone except his father, who just kind of shook his head, the light catching his silver hair. He exchanged a look with his uncle, who also shook his head.

"Well?" he asked.

Shane leaned forward, winked at him. "Seems you made a pass at your pretty doctor here."

His gaze shot to Ava. She just shrugged and, though

she tried to play it off, he could see her cheeks had turned red. So that was the reason for her sideways looks.

"It happens." She pasted a wide smile on her face. "Anesthesia makes people say some strange things." She started to inch backward. "So nice to meet everyone. I have to continue on my rounds."

She ducked out so fast, he looked around and said, "What did I supposedly say to her?"

Crystal laughed. His siblings all smiled. His dad and his uncle Bob were the only ones who didn't seem amused, but that wasn't uncommon for the elder Gillians. His uncle and dad could be twins when it came to temperament, except where his dad looked older and wrinkled with age, his Uncle Bob still looked the same. Bushy grey grows, thick mustache, face relatively unlined with age.

"You told her how hot she was and that you wanted to take her out on a date," Crystal said gleefully. "Apparently it's the talk of the hospital. I guess Dr. Moore is a bit of a stick in the mud and so everyone thought it was funny."

"She's not a stick in the mud. She's just overwhelmed by being a doctor and a mom and a single parent."

The whole room went quiet—well, as quiet as it could be given they were in a recovery room and other patients were within earshot. Even his dad quirked a brow.

"Well, well, well," said his aunt. "Look who's smitten."

She couldn't get out of there fast enough.

Things were out of hand as far as Carson Gillian was concerned and it irritated the heck out of her. Why did she always seem to fall for the cocky masculine type?

Fall?

Okay. So it was more like attracted. She paused in front of a window overlooking the parking lot of the hospital. In the distance, fluffy clouds left ink-blot shadows on the hills and the mountains to the west. She'd been flattered by his comments in the recovery room, although there was a part of her that had a hard time believing he'd meant them. He might have been hallucinating she was someone else.

The bummer of it was that she'd have to see him again in a few days, and after that, on the weekend when Bella had her riding lesson. For the first time she wished she had someone she could pass his chart along to, but that would be unprofessional at best, and cowardly without a doubt.

She managed to avoid him as he left the hospital later that day.

It didn't help that Bella couldn't seem to stop talking about her lesson that weekend. As she played with Balto in the kitchen later that same day, she even asked how his surgery had gone.

"Great," Ava said, hoping her daughter would drop it.

"Will he be able to ride again?"

"Sure, sure," she said dismissively, spooning some spaghetti onto her daughter's plate.

"I mean, will he be able to ride at rodeos again, Mom?"

Okay, she thought, taking a seat at the head of the square table, next to her daughter. She wasn't going to let the matter drop.

"I don't see why not."

She took a bite of her food, hoping Bella would do the same. She did. But the moment she finished chewing and swallowing, she was back at it again.

"I hope he does really good. When I met Carson's brother at the ranch he said he could go all the way." She sat straighter. "Maybe we could fly to Las Vegas and watch him ride."

"When did you meet his brother?"

"At the barn the other day." Bella smiled. "So can we go to Vegas?"

Not if she could help it. "How was school today?"

Bella launched into a play-by-play of how her day had gone. Ava tried to focus on her words but her thoughts kept slipping back to Carson. If he fell again, he might injure that elbow worse than before. She'd have to make sure he knew the risks. And that he didn't do too much too soon.

"Mom!"

Ava jerked. Balto whined from his position at Bella's feet. Bella stared up at her accusingly.

"I asked you if I could bring Rosa out to the ranch this weekend."

Rosa? Who was Rosa—a school friend? "We'll have to ask Carson first."

Bella stared up at her quietly. Ava didn't like the look on her face at all. It was far too knowing for someone her age.

"You like him, don't you?"

What? "Like who?" She pretended confusion.

"Carson."

"He's a patient, honey. Of course I like him."

That wasn't exactly true. She'd disliked plenty of the people she'd operated on over the years.

"Not like that," Bella said. She tipped her head sideways. Someone had braided her bangs and then clipped them off to the side. She wondered who'd done it…and how come she hadn't noticed before now.

"Every time you talk about him, your face turns red."

"It does not."

Bella nodded. "It does. And you're trying to change the subject."

Ava set her fork down. She didn't want to be having this conversation. "Finish your dinner." She glanced down at the puppy at her feet. "And stop feeding him scraps."

"Mom, why don't you ever go out on dates?"

Where was this coming from? Ava sat back in her chair, unsure how to answer. It was clear Bella had something she wanted to get off her chest. Her daughter had set her fork down, too.

"Honey, I'm too busy to do that. Besides, it'd be unprofessional. He's a patient."

"But he's had his surgery," she said, brown eyes wide.

"He's still my patient." For now. Once he started therapy, his care would be passed to someone else, but still.

Bella wasn't going to drop it. "You could ask someone else to be his doctor."

Her daughter was entirely too smart for her own good, and so very much like Paul. He'd seen the world in black-and-white, too.

"And that would be unprofessional." Ava shook her head. "So let's just drop it, shall we?"

She should have known better than to try to escape. Even when she got up to put her plate in the sink, Bella still hadn't picked up her fork again. She just kept staring at her to the point that Ava leaned back against the sink and said, "What?"

"Ask him out, Mom."

"I can't do that."

"Yes, you can. You're a strong, powerful woman. And women can do anything. That's what you always tell me."

It took her a moment to realize her mouth hung open. She closed it with a click of her teeth. "This is different."

Bella shook her head. "You need to have some fun, Mom. You're like that guy from that movie. You know, the one where his wife dies and he doesn't date anybody for, like, a really long time."

"What movie?"

"You know," Bella said impatiently. "The guy that

plays Forrest Gump. He's in it. And you always cry at the end. You're like him, except a girl."

It took her a moment to place the movie, and then she straightened in outrage. "*Sleepless in Seattle*? I am not."

"Face it, Mom. You're like that man, the one you called a lonely widower."

"Honey, it's not just that he's my patient. There are other reasons, too. Sometimes even when you like someone, you don't want to date them."

"So you admit you do like him." Bella pounded on the words like a cat on a butterfly.

"Not like that." Okay, maybe she did. A little. He was so good with Bella. "He's a really nice guy, but he's a rodeo cowboy, Bella."

"I know. It's cool."

Ava shook her head. "It wouldn't be cool when he was on the road all the time." Girls throwing themselves at him, no doubt. Look at all the hospital nurses. She could only imagine what it was like for him when he was out on the road. No thanks. "It's like spotting a cake at the market and knowing it looks good, but also knowing it'd be bad for you, so you don't eat it."

Bella frowned. "You're comparing Carson to cake?"

She knew when to stop arguing with her daughter. Bella wouldn't stop. She'd keep tossing out solution after solution until one of them gave up. This time around it was Ava.

"Finish your dinner," she said again, turning to leave the kitchen. "I'll be upstairs, folding laundry."

One day her daughter would understand, although she hoped that day was way far in the future. She couldn't imagine navigating the shoals of Bella's social life. The thought practically gave her hives.

When her cell phone dinged a little later she winced, hoping against hope she wasn't being called in to work. She wasn't. It was a text from Carson.

I hate to bug you, but my dad would like you to sign a release. He's worried about liability.

Liability? Well, yes she could understand that. But why did she want to delay her response?

She sat on the edge of her bed.

She did not want to get involved with him, not at all, and yet that didn't stop that little heart-tickling flutter whenever she thought about him and what he'd said in the recovery room. Not that he'd remembered.

Sure. I'll sign one when I'm out there this weekend.

She tipped her head back, finding it ridiculous that she waited with bated breath for his reply. It was like being a teenager all over again. She was just about to toss the phone aside when it dinged once more.

And if you wouldn't mind paying me then?

Oh, dear goodness. She'd forgotten to pay the man. Here she was talking about keeping things professional and she'd walked off without paying for his services.

Because you're not yourself when you're around him.

Okay, so maybe that was true, but it was time to take back control. She wasn't going to date the man, ever. She would treat him like the professional he was.

I can pay you now. And sign your release. Meet in town?

Her heart began to pump like a cardiac patient's just before a heart attack. Stupid and ridiculous, and all the more reason to prove to herself that she could handle

her attraction to Carson Gillian without feeling like a
silly schoolgirl.

Her phone dinged.

Sure. How about tomorrow? Name a time.

She'd sign his paper and hand him the money. What
better way to prove her professionalism.

Then why are you already plotting what to wear?

She refused to answer the question.

Chapter 8

Humiliating.

That was what it felt like to ask someone, especially an attractive someone, for money.

Carson stared into the coffee shop. The glass storefront reflected passing traffic behind him, but beyond the glass, inside the store, he could see a line of people at the counter.

It wasn't like he didn't have a savings account, and he'd made some good money at rodeos over the years, but now he was out of commission for who knew how long and he hated—actually, refused—to touch his construction savings account. One day he'd build his dream home on the back of his family's property, something that would belong to him, and not his dad or uncle. He'd buy the land from them, build the house, but not something that looked new. Oh, no. He'd always loved old houses for their woodwork and unique details. His house would look old, but be new on the inside. Until he could build it, though, he'd do what he needed to do to get by, and that included selling his services to his pretty new doctor and her daughter.

The smell of coffee greeted him the moment he opened the door and he could hear the whir of a coffee grinder. The place seemed to be packed this early in the day and, for a moment, Carson wondered if he'd even be able to find her. But there she sat, at a table in the far corner of the shop, a smile that seemed forced upon her face.

"Hey," he said, pulling out a metal chair that matched the table right down to the polished aluminum surface.

"You made it," she said.

He plopped down on the metal chair. "I did." He held up a file folder. "Here's the release we talked about. I'm sure you're going to want to read it. I'll just go get myself a cup of coffee while you do."

She leaned forward and picked up the folder, a stream of steam rising from an oversize coffee mug on the table. He could smell chocolate inside of whatever it was. That was the moment he realized she looked different. Her hair was down and curled. She wore a light-blue cotton shirt with a scooped neckline and sleeves that flared at the end. Earrings dangled from her ears.

Gorgeous.

"I'll be right back." He shot up out of his chair. "Gonna get myself that coffee." He turned away without another word. There were a million reasons why he should stay away from her, not the least of which being that she was his doctor. What kind of idiot would ever make a pass at the professional in charge of his care?

Your kind of idiot, a little voice answered.

He'd been drugged, though, so it didn't count, and she certainly seemed to have dismissed it. So would he.

He took his time ordering coffee, but he couldn't seem to stop himself from glancing over at her. She seemed engrossed in her task.

"This looks fine," she said when he returned, setting the paper down, reaching into her purse hanging off the back of her chair and pulling something out. His check. And a pen. He set his coffee down, watching as she signed her name on the bottom of the release before filling out her check.

"How much?"

Their eyes connected, a current of something passing between them. The same kind of something he felt whenever she touched him.

"I don't know. I've never given riding lessons before." He had to take a sip of his coffee. To look anywhere but at her. Something like embarrassment had him sipping a little too quickly, making him cough.

"You okay?"

"Fine."

"How does sixty dollars an hour sound?"

Sixty? That sounded like a lot. "I think half that would probably be more appropriate."

She studied him for a moment. "I think you're selling yourself too short."

Selling himself. Ha. Yeah. He supposed in a way he was, and it was no big deal. Lots of professional cowboys trained people to ride. Why the hell did it matter that she was paying him?

"Suit yourself."

She went back to filling out the check, passing it to him a moment later. "I paid you for six lessons."

Six. That was a few hundred dollars. "You didn't have to do that."

"I wanted to." She took a sip of her coffee. "So how do you think Bella's progressing?"

"Great," he said. "She's a natural."

She nodded. "She enjoys it."

"She could be good enough to show one day."

Her eyes held his own. "You think?"

"I do." He glanced around, wondering how quickly he could get out of there. It hit him then why he had such a hard time taking payment from her. It made him feel like a loser. As if he was some kind of poor cowboy living from paycheck to paycheck. And there she was, the big, successful doctor. It was emasculating.

"She'd be thrilled."

"She'll have to work hard."

"That might be good for her." There was so much hope in her voice that it caught his interest.

"Is she having trouble in school?"

A brow rose. "No." She inhaled deeply. "Nightmares. On and off for years. It's part of how we got started on this whole horse thing. I mean, she's always wanted one, but then I did some research and learned they're great emotional support animals."

"They are."

"So maybe the extra exercise and being loved by a horse will help out."

"I'm sure it will."

He studied her eyes, examining all the various shades of green as if he could find an answer to questions he didn't even know he was asking. He saw sadness in those eyes. And kindness. And curiosity.

"I really admire you."

Her eyes flickered. He jolted, too, because he hadn't expected to say the words out loud.

"Thank you."

In for a penny, in for a pound. "You're a hell of a role model for that little girl."

Did she blush? He was almost certain she did.

"I didn't have a choice."

"Yes, you did. A lot of people would have thrown in the towel after the death of a loved one."

Like he'd given up rodeo. But he didn't want to examine that thought too deeply.

"You could have given up school, found a job, walked

away from your dreams, but you didn't. That's pretty amazing."

Definitely a blush. He liked the way it emphasized her cheeks, and he wondered how anyone as pretty as Ava hadn't been snatched up by some wealthy businessman or a co-worker doctor. Someone the exact opposite of him.

He stood suddenly. "I'm going to get something to eat, too."

She nodded, eyes wide. "Okay," she said softly.

"Be right back."

He had to force himself to turn and head to the counter, but he had to leave. He needed to gather his wits and to breathe and to think. What the hell was he doing complimenting her like that? This wasn't a date. He was a part-time rodeo cowboy who made furniture for a living. She was a good-looking brainiac who made more in a month than he did all year. They were two complete opposites. She had a kid. A career. She probably didn't have a boyfriend because she didn't want or need one. Who needed a man when you had the world at your feet, especially a broken-down cowboy?

"Damn," he muttered.

So this was what it felt like to be smitten with someone?

He had a crush on his doctor.

"My, my, my," Ava heard a woman say as Carson came toward her with a plate in his good hand. He'd bought a muffin to go with his coffee.

My, my, my, the woman inside Ava silently agreed. The pragmatic part of her had to look away, horrified that she'd been ogling her patient.

A glance at the women around her revealed that every female eye in the immediate vicinity followed his prog-

ress back to their table, not surprising given he looked
about ready to burst out of his jeans. They clung to the
muscular build of his legs and hugged him in all the right
places. His black cowboy hat set off his dark eyebrows,
bringing his blue eyes to prominence. Something about
him being injured added to the allure. They'd fitted him
with a neoprene-and-Velcro brace that looked like some
kind of space-age armor. Two straps encircled his upper
arm with two similar straps below his elbow, the pieces
connected by a thick piece of metal on front and back
with a dial on the outside to control angles. He looked
like he'd been riding out on the range, maybe battling
with a bull, emerging the victor, but with a war wound.

Carson seemed oblivious. He smiled at her as he sat
and she wondered if people were speculating about what
the heck a plain Jane like her was doing with a hunk of
masculine cowboy like him.

"Is that a *bran* muffin?"

He glanced at his plate and she could have sworn she
spotted a look of surprise. "Why, I believe it is."

"Don't you know?"

"I just told them to give me whatever."

She smiled. "They must have thought you needed
something healthy."

"Guess so."

"How is your arm feeling?" That was better. Bring it
back to patient and doctor.

"It still aches a bit. I've been icing it, like the nurse
said, but it throbs from time to time."

"That's to be expected. Even though you got to go
home the same day, it was still major surgery."

"Yeah, about that…" He took a sip of his coffee. "I
don't know what got into me in the recovery room—"

"Don't mention it." *Please*, she silently urged. *Don't.*

"It really does happen. I once had a patient wake up who wouldn't stop singing the National Anthem. You should have heard him. Kept singing and singing at the top of his lungs. Nurses talked about it for weeks."

He smiled. She wondered if she should cut their visit short. Now that they'd conducted their business, there was really no need to hang around.

But she wanted to. Oh, how she wanted to. Something about being in the presence of a handsome male titillated her feminine side.

She gulped. "Anyway, you'll feel better each day. When do you start your therapy?"

"Next week." He looked as glum as someone forced into jury duty.

"It won't be as bad as you think." She wanted to touch his hand. Why did she always want to do that? "When they take your brace off, you'll be surprised at how good your elbow will feel. Well, it's going to hurt, don't get me wrong, but it's more of a bruising type of pain, not a deep bone-throbbing ache. Or so I've been told."

"Good to know." He smiled a little bigger. "I think."

She really should go. There was no reason to spend any more time with him than absolutely necessary.

"Thanks for meeting me this morning." She reached around and grabbed her purse. "I'm sorry I forgot to give you a check the other day. I'll see you this weekend for Bella's lesson."

He seemed surprised at the abrupt way she stood, but he didn't insist she stay and for that she was grateful.

"That's okay."

No, you're disappointed.

Okay, so maybe his easy acquiescence left her deflated. What red-blooded female wouldn't want to be seen in his company?

"Call me at the hospital if you develop any pain or redness at your incision sites."

"Will do."

Way to bring it back to patient and doctor. But as she walked out the door, part of her wondering if he watched her go, she wished she wasn't quite so sensible. And that he didn't remind her so much of Paul. And that he wasn't a patient.

Sometimes things just weren't meant to be.

Chapter 9

Ava barely spared him a glance as she waved goodbye, the scent of coffee reminding him that he had a drink to finish up. And a bran muffin. Although how the hell he'd ended up with one of those he had no idea.

"Well, well, well. Look who's here."

Carson almost groaned. Just what he needed. His sister, Jayden, was walking over to him from a nearby table. He hadn't seen her since she'd snuck in to visit him in the hospital, a complete surprise given she'd told him she'd call.

"And was that Dr. Moore I saw with you?"

He tried to paste on a blank expression before looking up at her. His sister's blue eyes followed Ava's progress to her car. He saw her lips twitch just before she faced him. "I've heard of house calls, but not coffeehouse calls."

It was hard not to roll his eyes. "Ha, ha, ha. Very funny. We were just signing some paperwork. Dad got worried about liability, so I had her sign a release. Plus, she owed me money."

Her eyes dimmed at the mention of their father and he inwardly kicked himself. Usually he avoided the *dad* word. Reese Gillian had disowned his daughter when she'd gotten pregnant out of wedlock, something none of them approved of or understood, but Jayden had done okay for herself. Still, he knew it hurt.

"Don't *you* owe *her* money for your surgery?"

"I don't know. Insurance is paying for it, I think."

Her gaze caught on his splint. "How's the arm?"

"Good," he said with a deep breath, happy for the change of subject and hoping she was dropping the issue of Dr. Moore. "For now. No reaction to the hardware. Incision looks good, too. Supposed to go in for yet another X-ray next week, see how things are healing. Physical therapy is next."

Jayden's eyes went back to teasing him again. "Will you see your favorite doctor then?"

"I doubt it. She doesn't have anything to do with physical therapy, and I don't think she does radiology."

Jayden set her purse on the table and took a seat opposite him. He didn't want her to. He had a feeling his little sister was about to assume the role of mother and grill him. She was good at that.

"What?" he asked.

She watched Ava drive away before focusing on him. "She's a single mom, Carson."

Tell him about it. "It's not like that."

"So you say, but you should be careful. Dating her won't be the same as dating one of your rodeo fans."

"I'm not going to date her."

She tipped her head to the side, a gesture so reminiscent of his mother that for a moment it was hard to swallow. Jayden looked like her, too, except with dark hair. His mom had been such a beauty.

"She has a daughter."

For the love of…

"Sis, really. Stop. It's not like that."

"So you said. But you clearly like her a little more than a patient should. At least you did when you were waking up from anesthesia, or so I heard from Aunt Crystal."

"That wasn't me. Well, I mean, it was me." He shrugged.

"And, okay. She's pretty. I'll give you that, but you remember Kat."

She shivered. "Unfortunately."

"It's the same kind of deal. You wouldn't believe the drive Dr. Moore has. Did you know she raised her daughter all on her own? Put herself through medical school without any help from family. She has no family. She's done it all solo, kind of like you."

Jayden cocked a brow, the left side of her mouth lifting in a smirk. "You admire her."

"Well, yeah. Don't you? But that's not my point. My point is she's a woman who's dedicated to her career. And her daughter. No room for a man, and certainly not a man like me."

"Hmm. If you say so."

He wasn't surprised Jayden would mention her concerns. She lived the life of a single mom. His niece, Paisley, was three years old. But Jayden hadn't let her teenage pregnancy her from going on to college and getting a degree in sports medicine. In a lot of ways, Jayden reminded him of Ava, just a younger version.

Still, he'd watched his sister over the years, admired her for all she'd been through. His dad hadn't made her life easy. He could have offered her a place to live on the ranch, could have helped support her, but he was notoriously tough on his kids, and even harder on his only daughter. He'd hoped that would change after his heart surgery, but he hadn't let up. So they all tried to help out with Paisley when they could, his Aunt Crystal more than anybody, but he wondered if Jayden missed being carefree, and if maybe she regretted getting pregnant at such a young age.

"*You* should be dating more."

"Don't change the subject."

He almost laughed. His sister gave him "the look." The one that was so much like their mother's—right down to the wrinkles that formed between her two eyes—that it sobered him for a moment.

"She reminds me of you, honestly. You both have the same kind of drive."

"And that's *my* point. You and I both know you prefer women that are a little more…" She bit her lip as she tried to choose a word. "Free."

"Free?" He shook his head. "What's that supposed to mean? I'm not dating mustangs or something."

"You know what I mean. The women in your life come and go, and there's nothing wrong with that. It's not like you're out there breaking hearts like *some* people we know."

She meant Levi. The man who'd left her high and dry once she'd gotten pregnant.

"The women you date know the drill. You do, too. But dating Dr. Moore? That would be different."

"All right." He held up a hand. "Enough."

"Don't be offended. I don't think you're a jerk about it or anything. Like I said, they all know you're a player—"

"A player!"

"No. Not really a player. That was the wrong word." It was her turn to be the uncomfortable one. "How do I say this? Carson, you're a big, lovable teddy bear. Women adore you. But the minute they start making demands, you let them down—even the hideous Katarina." She lifted her hands to curtail his denial. "Gently. You don't dump them like some kind of loser. You make jokes about your dating phobia—your words—and sweet talk them, and sometimes you even make them think it's their idea to break up. It's kind of genius, and I've seen it happen at least half a dozen times over the years."

She made him sound like a regular ladies' man. "It might surprise you to know that I'd already decided she wasn't my type," he quipped.

Jayden admonished him with a frown. "Anything with legs is your type."

"Hey."

She smiled to take the sting out of her words. "And anyway, since when have you ever had a 'type'?"

Okay. So she had him there. "I do respect her, though. I can't deny it."

Jayden leaned back, studying him for a while. "Enough to stop flirting with all the pretty girls on the rodeo circuit? To go home after a rodeo and not out to a dance? To commit to not just Ava but her daughter, too? Can you do all that?"

Of course he could. But he didn't answer, just stared at his hands. "I don't know what all the fuss is about," he grumbled. "I doubt she even thinks of me as more than an annoying patient that just so happens to give her daughter riding lessons."

Jayden snorted. "Yeah, right. Don't tell me you haven't gotten to the ripe old age of twenty-nine without realizing the effect you have on women. Never understood why. Must be the cowboy hat, but I assure you, Dr. Moore's not blind."

"She's not stupid, either."

"What does that mean?"

"Just that I'm sure she knows I'm not up to her standard, educationwise. She could have anybody, not a broken old cowboy that's never done much with his life."

"You made it to the National Finals Rodeo," his sister said. "That's not exactly nothing."

"Yeah, but I wasn't even trying to make it," he said, thinking back on his stint at the NFR.

"And why is that?" Jayden asked. "Why haven't you tried a little harder?"

"I just didn't care."

Jayden's eyes grew wide. "Wow. Don't let Dad hear that."

"Dad would be the first to tell you I lacked the passion. He would be right, too, but not anymore. I'm turning over a new leaf. This injury was a huge wake-up call. You never appreciate something until it's taken away from you."

"So—" Jayden leaned forward "—get your act together, Carson." She leaned further toward him. "Go out and make it to the finals. Hell, win the average. Win the world. Like I've told Aunt Crystal, you're so much better than you think you are. You're every bit Dr. Moore's equal. Don't you think otherwise. But that doesn't mean I think the two of you could work out. You're not ready for an instant family, especially if you're going to make a run for the NFR, and I hope you do. One thing at a time, big brother."

She stood, moved to kiss him on the cheek beneath his cowboy hat. "Why don't you come over for dinner one night this week?" she asked.

"Sure." He leaned back. "Not like I have much else to do."

She flicked his hat brim. "Now don't you go feeling all sorry for yourself. You'll be back out there again. You'll see."

He hoped she was right. But as she walked away, his thoughts returned to her concerns and, against his better judgment, he found himself wondering what it might be like to date Ava. Just as soon as he had the thought, he dismissed it, though. No way would she ever date a guy like him. And no way was it the right time for him to be getting involved with a woman like her.

That was the one thing he was sure of.

It didn't stop him from thinking about her for the rest of the week, though. Or from being on edge the morning of Bella's lesson. So when Bella arrived for her lesson alone, he was almost disappointed.

"Where's your mom?"

Bella stopped, rested her hand on her thigh, her riding tights the same color as her shirt. Blue.

"I think she's trying to avoid you."

Carson felt his cowboy hat lift with his brows. "What do you mean?"

"She just about booted me from the car today and when I asked her if she wanted to watch me ride, she said she didn't need to. That I'd progressed enough that she didn't worry about me anymore—and we both know that's a crock. She still tries to make me wear floaties in the pool."

The little girl looked so irritated Carson wanted to laugh, probably would have if he hadn't been so...so...-

Disappointed.

Less than a half hour with him and she'd already written him off. Figured.

"So what's going on with you two?"

Wait a minute. Who was the kid and who was the adult? "Nothing." He thought back. "We had coffee. She signed a release so you can ride and gave me a check for your lessons and then she left."

Quickly, and for the first time, he wondered about that.

Bella crossed her arms, what looked like a brand-new hard hat dangling off the crook of her elbow. "Well I think she likes you."

"No."

"Yes."

Suddenly he wanted to laugh. "Are you sure you're only nine?"

She shrugged a shoulder. "My mom says I'm mature for my age because I'm an only child." She shook her head. "All I know is I don't need to be grown up to know she's acting weird."

Not because of him. At least, he didn't think so. And even if Ava did sort of fancy him, it didn't mean anything. But how to explain to Bella that sometimes people didn't want to date one another because they were just too different? Despite what Jayden had said, Ava was a city-raised doctor who'd just so happened to move to Via Del Caballo. He was a country boy who spent a lot of his life on the road when he wasn't building furniture. A doctor and a cabinetmaker. What a couple.

"I don't think I'm her type," he admitted.

Bella's arms dropped to her sides. In the middle of the aisle, studying him so intently, her head tilted slightly to one side, she reminded him so much of Ava. Hard to believe they weren't related by blood. Must be the mannerisms.

"I want her to be happy." The girl looked so intense and so determined that Carson felt his heart twinge. How was he supposed to respond to that?

"She tries to pretend as if her life is perfect but I hear the way she sighs when she watches romance movies. You should have seen her during the Hallmark Christmas movie marathon. She went through three boxes of tissues. And then she'll say something like—" she lowered her voice "—'only in the movies.'" Bella rolled her eyes. "I don't think she likes it here as much as I do and I worry she'll want to move. And if that happens…"

It'd break her heart. The kid was horse crazy. Funny

how that happened. Born in a city but with a love of the animals he cherished, too.

"How's Balto?" he asked.

She smiled. "He's good. Sleeps with me every night. Drives Mom crazy because she spent a ton of money on that kennel, but I just go grab him every night. And I don't mind cleaning up after him. And don't change the subject."

Good Lord. The kid could take a page out of his sister's book.

"She likes you and she doesn't ever like any man."

That was flattering, but Bella was only nine years old. There could be some other reason her mom was acting strange.

"What if you call her and tell her I fell off? She'd have to come here and talk to you."

"Bella. No. You're not going to do that."

Bella wrinkled her nose. "Yeah. You're probably right." She crammed her helmet onto her head. "Let me think about this while I ride. I'll go get Little Red."

"Actually—" he was glad to change the subject "—I thought you could ride one of the show horses today."

"Really?" She spoke the word so loudly she startled the sorrel in the stall behind her.

"You've got a natural seat, Bella. And a real feel for a horse's mouth. And Snazzy is easy to ride. Super broke. You should have no problem handling her."

He led her to Snazzy's stall. The mare was a bay with four white socks. Older, but still bright eyed and curious about the little girl who cooed and awed over her.

She doesn't ever like any man...

Stop it, he told himself. It didn't mean a hill of beans.

"She looks just like one of my model horses," Bella said.

"Oh, yeah?"

Bella led the mare out of her stall. "My favorite one. You should see my collection. It's huge."

Horse crazy for sure. But he had to give her credit. She'd picked up quickly on how to saddle and bridle a horse. The mare seemed genuinely interested in her young rider, turning her head to look at her and then nudge her.

Carson forgot about his troubles with Ava as he watched Bella put on leg boots and bell boots. When she climbed aboard in a few moments without even using a mounting block, and then later began to put the mare through her paces out in the arena, the two of them seemed to click and Carson knew he was on to something good.

"All right, I'm going to work you on the flag. Gonna need you to hang on because once she realizes what we're doing, she's going to move around fast. Don't fall off."

Bella nodded, a serious look on her face beneath the helmet she wore. Daylight faded for a moment as the sun disappeared behind a cloud. Looked like rain later on, he thought, crossing to the switch that controlled a wire that stretched down the long side of the arena, a bright orange flag in the middle. Pulleys would tug the wire left and right, Snazzy having been trained to follow the movement.

"You ready?" he asked.

Bella nodded.

The horse must have heard the machine kick to life because she dropped her head and ducked right.

Bella gasped and then giggled, then hung on to the horn because Snazzy shot to the left, this time galloping a few strides to keep up with the flag's movement, only to stop suddenly when it shifted right, faster this time so that Snazzy cantered longer. Bella laughed and hung on, the smile on the kid's face doing something to Carson's insides. Back they went, the girl's giggles filling the air, both hands clutching the saddle horn, the reins forgotten in her hands.

"Hang on," he said when Snazzy shifted left-right a little too quickly. His hand hovered over the switch, ready to shut it off, but Bella was giggling and laughing and, damn, if she didn't hang on.

"That's it," he said with pride. He reached for his hat, pulling it off and waving it her way in approval. "Way to go, Bella."

He shut the machine off. The horse instantly stopped. Bella sat there in the saddle laughing and wiping at her eyes now that she could let go.

"Oh my gosh, Carson, that was *so* much fun."

"It is, isn't it?"

"Can I do it again?"

"Let's give Snazzy a little break first. Why don't you walk her around a bit? Let her catch her breath."

They both turned, Carson drawing up short.

"Mommy!" Bella's cry of delight could probably be heard all the way up at his dad's house on the hill behind them. "Did you see me? Did you?" She kicked Snazzy toward the rail.

"I did," Ava said, and something sounded funny about her voice. It took Carson a moment to realize what it was. She was crying.

His heart flipped over in his chest for a whole other reason.

"Why are you crying?" Bella asked.

Carson saw Ava wipe her cheeks, watched as she took a deep breath and looked up at her daughter. "Because, honey, that's the first time I've heard you laugh like that in a long, long time." And then she looked past her daughter and into Carson's eyes. *Thank you*, she mouthed.

You're welcome, he mouthed back.

And Carson knew Bella was right. There was something there. Something that hung in the air between them and made him feel like he sat in a ride at a carnival, one that went up and down and did loops and spins and that made it hard to concentrate for a moment.

What the hell?

He couldn't figure it out, didn't know if he even wanted to figure it out. All he knew was that making Ava happy made *him* happy.

That was the craziest thing of all.

Chapter 10

She should have stuck to her original plan. Should have stayed away until Bella's allotted one-hour lesson was up and then waited for her in front of the stables. Instead she'd stood by the side of the arena and watched as Carson worked with her daughter, made Bella laugh, which made Ava cry.

She deserved this.

For so many years it'd been nose to the grindstone. Finally they were able to reap the benefits of all their hard work. And for Ava it culminated in the moment she'd watched Bella throw her head back and laugh like she hadn't laughed in forever.

"That's good right there," Carson called out. "I think Snazzy's had enough for one day."

"Aw, man." Bella's disappointment was unmistakable, her shoulders slumping, a pout tugging at the edges of her mouth.

"Next weekend," Carson said, "we'll ride a little longer. As it is, you're going to be sore tomorrow."

"I already am," Bella said proudly, turning her horse to the gate. "Mom, did you see that last time Snazzy shot back to the right?" She mimicked the motion with her hand. "Pffft. Off she went." The smile came back to Bella's face.

Carson came up next to her. Their gazes met and, for what seemed like the thousandth time, she tried not to notice what a good-looking man he was in his white T-shirt and black cowboy hat. He always seemed poured into his clothes and it didn't seem fair to the opposite sex that he could be so handsome and so damn nice, too. Not fair at all.

"She's doing great," he said with a wide smile. He had perfect teeth, too.

"She looks good."

"Mom," Bella said, "can Carson come over for dinner tonight?"

She froze. Carson seemed to straighten in surprise, too. Ava opened her mouth. Nothing came out of it.

"You could make that mac and cheese I love so much." Bella twisted in her saddle so she could face Carson. "She makes the best homemade mac and cheese. The best."

"I don't think—"

"Bella, no," Carson said at the same time Ava spoke. They glanced at each other in surprise before facing Bella again. At least they were on the same page.

"Tonight's not a good night—" she improvised "—I have to work in the morning."

"So?" Bella pulled up Snazzy. "I'll do the dishes and stuff. All you'd have to do is make the meal. It'll be perfect."

"Actually I have plans," Carson said.

Bella sat straighter in the saddle. "Doing what?"

"Bella." Ava had never been more horrified in her life. "It doesn't matter what he's doing. He gave you an answer."

"Fine." Bella tipped her chin up. "Come over now. We'll have the mac and cheese for lunch."

"Bella…"

"Mom, it's the least we can do. Carson has been so nice to us. And you're always telling me to be nice to people in return, right?"

"Well, I—"

"Please, you guys. I want to show Carson my collection of model horses, too. Please? Carson, I know you're not busy because you told me you were going to grab takeout after my lesson and eat it here."

They'd been outmaneuvered. Carson looked at her. She shrugged. If she protested any more, she'd seem like a spoilsport, or worse, a big chicken, because Carson was looking at her strangely.

He knew. The damn man had figured out she had a crush on him. Worse, it amused him. Well, he would see she was made of sterner stuff.

"Sure," she said brightly. "Why not?"
There. Take that.

"You don't mind, do you, Mom?" Bella asked as she all but thrust herself inside the SUV. She pulled the door closed and turned to face her. "I mean, I think it's the least we can do. He let me ride a show horse today, Mom. A *real* show horse. And he said I could compete on her, but first he wants us to go watch one. There's a horse show in another week. It's the kind the Gillians do. A National Cutting Horse Association show. Can we go?"

It was hard to feel put out when Bella was clearly thrilled with life. This was what she'd wanted for her daughter…only without Carson.

Carson.

"Sure, honey. We can go."

How the heck had the man figured it out? Had it been her hasty retreat from the coffee shop? She'd all but run out of there. How humiliating that he had, though. It meant she'd have to be on her guard. She couldn't risk someone like him slipping beneath her defenses.

"And you don't really mind him coming over, do you? You always say how easy it is to cook mac and cheese."

It was easy. And she loved cooking things from scratch. She took pride in ensuring Bella ate right. In her line of work she'd seen the effects of bad eating habits and what it could do to someone's health.

"I don't mind," she lied.

"Carson can tell us if he thinks Balto's gotten bigger. And I can show him how I've taught him to sit already and play fetch. And I really do want him to see my collection of model horses. There's one in there that looks just like the horse I rode today."

Ava didn't think tossing a ball and having the puppy bring it back some of the time qualified as an official game of fetch, but Bella was pleased with her puppy. Truth be told, there'd been a noticeable improvement in Bella's attitude ever since she'd started riding lessons and brought Balto home. She'd been nightmare-free, too, ever since that first night when she'd crawled into bed with her. She should have really put her foot down about the dog sleeping in the kennel, but she hadn't had the heart, and now she wondered if having the puppy sleeping next to her every night wasn't part of the cure, but whatever it was, she was relieved.

So suck it up, Ava told herself. It wouldn't be all that bad. It was the least she could do after everything he'd done for Bella. That was what she told herself.

And then she got home and decided that the shirt she wore looked wrinkled, so she changed it. Then she noticed a speck of dirt on her jeans, so she changed into a pair of black capris. And then her hair looked a mess, so she brushed it and maybe even dabbed on some lipstick, all the while calling herself the worst sort of fool. Carson would see right through her.

"You look nice," Bella said with a wide smile.

"My clothes were dirty."

Her brow furrowed. "Uh, Mom. You looked just fine to me." Bella turned away before she could comment.

"Where are you going?"

"I'm going to set the table."

Ava stood there in shock for a moment. Bella ignored her, pulling out some plates all the while whistling under her breath.

So that was how the wind blew? Her daughter liked Carson. Dear goodness. Bella wanted them to go out. That was the only way to explain why Bella happily chirped away, Balto at her feet. She debated with herself whether or not to set the record straight about any future romantic prospects with the man, but now was not the time. So Ava browned some onions and garlic and then mixed in cream and cheddar cheese and dry mustard for the sauce.

The doorbell rang. They both froze.

Bella said, "He's here," running for the door. Balto, thinking it a new game, tore off after her, puppy claws scrambling on the hardwood floor, ears bouncing up and down with every step.

Just smile and be polite. Just because your daughter's trying to be a matchmaker doesn't mean you have to go along with her plans.

"Hey, there," she heard him say from down the hall. "And look at Balto. I can't believe how much he's grown."

"Do you think so?" she heard Bella say, the two voices getting closer. "I know he's getting heavier, but I wasn't sure if he's any bigger."

Brace yourself.

"For sure he is," he said, coming into the kitchen.

And the damn man hadn't changed out of his work

clothes, which meant he smelled like outdoors and horses and some kind of masculine cologne that reminded her of a forest, and it was all she could do not to gawk. Why couldn't he be wearing a baggy T-shirt and pants? And how in the heck did he get such a tight shirt over his splint? And why the heck was she so irritated he hadn't changed when the man had to go back to work after lunch?

"Wow." His eyes swept to the oven beneath the cook-top where she'd just put the mac and cheese. "It smells amazing in here."

The flush of feminine pride made the tips of her ears go hot. "Thanks."

"Wait until you taste it," Bella said. Balto clattered around at her feet, his big brown eyes trained on the girl he already loved. "It's sooo good. My mom is an amazing cook."

"Really?" he asked with a lift of his eyebrows, his cowboy hat shifting upward, too. "Why am I not surprised?"

"She can sew, too. Not just with a needle and thread and stuff, but with a sewing machine and everything. She makes me a Halloween costume every year."

Ava's pleasure faded. It was so patently obvious what Bella was doing. Her cheeks were probably the same color as the rose petals in the stained-glass window in the family room. Probably glowed like them, too.

Carson's lips twitched before he said, "Sounds like she's a regular Betty Crocker." Clearly he knew what Bella was up to and he wasn't upset by it. If anything, he seemed benevolent about the whole thing. Like someone who was in on a joke, but only laughed because he was expected to. He probably had women fall at his feet all the time. Not here, though. Nope. Wasn't going to happen.

"She's really smart, too. But you probably already knew that. Graduated at the top of her class. She had her pick of jobs when she became a doctor, but she chose here so we could live in the country."

"Okay, that's enough." Ava hoped like heck he didn't think she'd put Bella up to this. "I'm sure Carson is tired of hearing all about me."

"No, it's okay."

It was definitely *not* okay and he knew it. He was just being polite, something her daughter would understand when she was older.

"I'm going to run up and go do homework."

Ava couldn't keep the surprise off her face. "What homework?"

"Just some math." Bella patted her leg. "Come on, Balto."

And now she'd left them alone. Ava wanted to close her eyes.

"So should I ask you to marry me right now or what?"

She wished the floor would open up and swallow her whole. "I'm so sorry."

He took a step closer to her and there it went again. Her heart, it just thumpity-thump-thumped in her chest. Why did it always do that when he stood so near?

"Don't be," he said. "I think it's cute."

"I should go have a talk with her."

"No, it's okay." He almost looked flattered. "Don't spoil her fun."

"We can't encourage her, though," she said quickly. "No matter what she might think, technically, you're still my patient."

He stared at her a long time and Ava grew more and more warm the longer she held his stare. Lord have mercy on her soul, something about the man made her feel like a teenager all over again.

"Oh, hey. Before I forget. I've got something for you." He left the kitchen and she damn near clutched the counter for support. This was getting out of hand.

"What do you think?" he said a moment later, dragging in with one arm…

A rocking chair?

He stopped in the middle of the kitchen. "When I was over here the other day, I noticed your family room was kind of barren."

Yes, it was. "It's a big house." And she never seemed to have time to go furniture shopping.

"I know. But I had this lying around. I made it for someone but they never paid me for it, so I started to think you could probably use it more than me. I remembered you telling me Bella had nightmares and I thought it'd be perfect for when she's upset. You know, to rock her to sleep and what not."

She stared at him mutely. It was probably the sweetest gift anyone had ever given her. Her heart pounded as she fought to hold back emotions.

"Thank you."

He shrugged. "No big deal. I'll put it in the family room for now."

A rocking chair. What kind of man gave a woman a rocking chair?

She shook her head, turned back to the kitchen and cleaning up, and to her surprise she felt her eyes begin to burn. It'd been so long since a man had done something nice for her.

So very, very long.

She felt more than saw him return. He was probably leaning against the counter like some kind of cowboy pin-up guy. Unfortunately her kitchen wasn't terribly big. Her Realtor had told her that was to be expected in older homes when kitchens were for servants, not families. It had never bothered her before…until now.

"Do you need any help?" he asked.

She stuffed the pot she'd just washed into the dishwasher. "No, no. Just sit down. We'll be eating in less than a half hour."

He didn't move. She forced herself to face him.

"You know, it's okay to let me help."

She didn't think it was possible for skin to feel as if it were burning, as in literally on fire, but that sure was what it felt like.

"I know." She shrugged. "I'm just used to doing things on my own."

He moved toward her. She told herself not to move even though she wanted to press back against the counter.

"Why is that?" He took another step closer. "Why don't you have someone in your life?"

You are a grown woman, Ava. You don't need to be intimidated by him.

"Because the older you get, the less you believe in fairy tales."

He stopped right in front of her. "That's so sad."

"It's reality."

"Don't you ever wonder what it might be like to forget the real world for a little while and to just let go?"

No. She worked in a vocation where things were often black-and-white, life-and-death. She couldn't afford the luxury of a fantasy life.

Liar.

She'd fantasized about him. Right after they'd had coffee, she'd had a dream. A good one. It'd woken her up in the middle of the night and then immediately filled her with embarrassment.

She tipped her chin up. "I'm a little more grounded than that."

"That's sad, too."

She started to shake her head. A hand brushed her jawline. She gasped.

"What are you doing?"

"I don't know," he said softly. "I keep telling myself to stay away from you, but here I am."

She gulped. "I feel the same way."

"And the craziest thing of all is I want to kiss you right now."

Yes. She wanted that, too. It must have been that damn chair. It'd weakened her resolve.

"You're my patient." It was all she could think to say.

"Then maybe you could fix my broken heart."

His broken heart? He'd had his heart broken? When?

But he didn't bend down. Didn't move. Didn't do anything but stare into her eyes, and she knew he was waiting for her to move away. He was giving her an out...if she wanted it. But it was time to admit she didn't want an out. She wanted him no matter how crazy it was and how unprofessional and how much she worried that this might lead to a place she didn't want to go. He smelled so good. And he was so damn good-looking. So when he slowly bent down, she closed her eyes.

His lips touched her own.

She went limp. She wanted so much more than a kiss from him. She wanted his hands and his body and his touch and his kisses. All of it. Something she hadn't had in so, so long.

He tipped his head sideways and she did, too, and when he increased the pressure she opened her mouth and thought she might fall to the floor. His left arm wrapped around her, pulling her close to him, his tongue testing the feel of her lips before slipping between them. And it was heaven, just heaven. She felt his left hand touch her side, a part of her careful not to move because she wouldn't want to hurt him.

At least, that was what she told herself.

She groaned. He might have moaned, too, but all too quickly he let her go.

She turned her back to him, rested her hands against the kitchen counter, tried to get her bearings.

Dear goodness.

"Wow," he said.

Yes, wow.

"If I'd known it would be like that, I would have kissed you days ago."

He'd wanted to kiss her days ago?

She whipped around, rested her backside against the countertop. "We can't do that again."

"I know."

He knew?

"I know you would never date a man like me."

Date a man like him? What did he mean? She examined his eyes, surprised to see disappointment in his own gaze.

A man like him. A man like Paul. Someone who had rocked her world and swept her off her feet before she'd had time to think. But she couldn't afford to not think about things now. She had Bella. And a career. And, God help her, a life she'd carved out for herself with hard work and determination. A man like Carson was the last thing she needed. Someone who flitted from rodeo to rodeo. Who seemed to live life by the seat of his pants. Dear goodness, he still lived at home.

"This has nothing to do with what kind of man you are."

Liar. It had everything to do with that. "Let's just forget this ever happened."

The oven dinged. Saved by the bell.

Chapter 11

He'd kissed her. Why the hell had he kissed her? And then to go and whine about how he wasn't her kind of man, like he was some kind of insecure idiot low on self-esteem. Humiliating.

"Lunch ready?" Bella said, breezing into the room.

"It is," Ava said brightly. Too brightly.

Bella skidded to a stop. "What happened?"

He found himself glancing at Ava. She refused to meet his gaze. "Nothing." She waved her daughter to the table. "Let's sit down and eat. That way, Carson can be on his way. I'm sure he has lots of work to do this afternoon."

He did. If it wouldn't have been rude, he would have seized that excuse and left right now.

"I never did see your model horses."

Bella brightened. "You didn't. Mom, can I take him upstairs and show him real quick?"

Ava couldn't have looked more relieved. "Sure. That'll give the mac and cheese time to cool."

They were barely out of earshot, heading upstairs, when Bella said, "Okay, what did you do?"

He damn near missed a step.

"She has the same look on her face as when I forget to take out the garbage."

He clutched the rail with his good hand. "I gave her a rocking chair."

It wasn't exactly a lie and it served its purpose. Bella

stopped on the stairs. He'd climbed a few before he realized it then stopped and stared down at her.

"You gave her a rocking chair?"

He shrugged. Honestly, he had no idea why he'd done it. He'd just seen it sitting in his workshop the other day and thought, *Why not?*

Why not, indeed. The look on her face. It'd done something to his insides.

"I think my gift took her by surprise."

That was true, too, and Bella seemed to accept it as a reasonable explanation for what had happened.

He took his time looking at the horses in Bella's collection. It gave him time to compose himself. Ava, too, by the looks of it. When they entered the kitchen again she had a smile on her face.

"Ready to eat?"

A phone rang.

Bella froze. So did he. Ava dashed for the phone on the counter, a look of dismay on her face.

"It's the ER," she said just before she picked up. "Dr. Moore."

They both watched her listen to the caller.

"There goes lunch," Bella muttered.

Was that what happened around here? One ring of the phone and off they went?

"I'll be right in."

When Ava turned to face them, Bella's shoulders slumped. "I'll go get my backpack."

"I need to go change," Ava told him.

"Is there anything I can do?"

Ava shook her head. "I'm sorry."

No, she wasn't. She was grateful for the interruption. Work had called her in and it was all the excuse she needed to dash off.

"Does Bella go into work with you?"

She shook her head, placing a hand on Bella's shoulders. "I have an older woman who watches her on days like today."

"But she hasn't eaten."

"I'll pack her some of the mac and cheese to go. And for you."

Bella stared at the floor, her happy smile gone now, disappointment dulling her eyes.

"Look." Carson told himself to leave it alone, to just leave, but he couldn't seem to stop himself from saying "Why don't you let me take her back to the ranch? She can help me muck stalls since I'm a little handicapped right now. You could swing by and pick her up afterward."

"Oh, Mom! Can I?"

The way Bella's face brightened... Well, it made his discomfort with the idea fade. He couldn't imagine having to go to the babysitter's all the time while your mom went off to work. It must be tough.

"You know how much I hate staying with Mrs. Crenshaw," Bella added.

Yes, her mom did know, Carson could see it on Ava's face. She couldn't hide her guilt even though he suspected she tried.

"I don't know."

"Pleeezzz," Bella begged. "Mrs. Crenshaw doesn't even have internet."

Ava nibbled her bottom lip. She glanced at her daughter then at him. "You sure it won't be a problem?"

"Not at all. Heck, it might even be good for her. A little hard labor never harmed a kid."

It must have reminded her of their conversation about

Bella's sleeping issues, and it broke through the last brick of her resistance.

"Okay." Ava looked into Bella's pleading eyes and nodded. "Fine. But if there's a problem with having her there, you have to promise to let me know."

"It won't be a problem." He tried to tell her with his eyes to let him help her out. That it was okay to depend on him for something.

You don't have to do this alone, he reminded her with his eyes.

Yes, I do, she silently answered back. Not this. Watching Bella, she would allow him to do, but he could tell by the look in her eyes that anything more than that would never happen again.

He turned away before she could see his disappointment.

Chapter 12

She was exhausted. Ava leaned against the counter in the staff kitchen and wondered how she'd be able to drive home. Not just one trauma patient had greeted her at the hospital, but six—all victims of a car crash. Two from one vehicle. Four from another. She'd had to call Carson and explain that it might be a late night. He'd reassured her that it was no problem. Bella had befriended his aunt and uncle and they were only too happy to let her spend the night there. Bella had been ecstatic at the thought of waking up and having horses within walking distance.

So she'd gone to work on an open compound fracture that'd nicked the femoral artery. A shattered foot that she feared would never be the same. Two other compound fractures that, thankfully, hadn't ruptured through the skin. Not open, but still required setting and one of them pins. Some other broken bones, ribs, a cracked vertebra. Worse, three of her patients had been children. Damn drunk drivers.

"Oh, there you are."

Ava looked up. Nurse Diaz greeted her with a smile.

"You have a surprise visitor." She pointed over her shoulder to the fluorescent-lit hallway beyond. "Something about your daughter insisting he bring you dinner."

Carson. Doing Bella's bidding, no doubt. It didn't surprise her. She'd have to put the kibosh on Bella's silly schoolgirl fantasies about the two of them hitting it off.

Tonight was proof of why things would never work out between them. Two people constantly being pulled apart by their commitment to their careers would never work. Geez, the only reason he was in town tonight was thanks to his injury. What about later?

Nope. Wasn't going to happen.

"Tell him I'll be right there."

The nurse nodded, and her purple scrubs with yellow smiley faces should have made Ava smile. She could barely summon the energy to do more than lift a hand in thanks. She had no idea how she'd summoned the energy to change into her street clothes. What a blessing Carson had taken Bella, though. That, she wouldn't deny. She would have hated to pick her up at this late hour. Poor kid had to put up with so much being her daughter. Perhaps that was why Ava spoiled her so much. Guilt.

For some reason the sight of Carson sitting in the waiting area wearing a fancy black shirt and a matching cowboy hat made her stumble a bit. He'd changed. Maybe shaved, too. It drew her up short.

"How long have you been here?"

He smiled wryly. "An hour or so." He motioned to the paper bag sitting on a chair next to him. "Compliments of my aunt Crystal. Everyone insisted I bring you dinner."

Did he hear the way her stomach growled at the mention of food? She hadn't eaten the mac and cheese she'd made for lunch. No time. Her hands shook, she was so hungry and exhausted.

"You look ready to drop," he said, standing. "Maybe I should drive you home."

She shook her head. "You don't have to do that." But a part of her wished he would scoop her up in his arms and carry her away, and that was so completely opposite of her normal way of thinking that it took her aback. She wasn't the kind that ever needed rescuing. She could take care of herself. Always had.

"Come on," he said, turning to pick up the bag. "We'll pick up your car tomorrow."

"No, really. It's okay."

He released a sigh. "And if you crash on the way home? If you fall asleep behind the wheel? What then?"

He had a point, but that didn't make her any less anxious to be alone with him. "It's only a little ways away. I'll be fine."

"Then I'll follow you home."

She was too exhausted to argue anymore. Her feet even felt heavy.

The cold night air hit her square in the face. Fog had rolled in while she'd been inside. And as always happened, it was strange to walk outside and realize it'd gotten dark. Midnight was less than a half hour away. Maybe she'd turn into a pumpkin. She'd like that. She could sleep in the pumpkin patch.

He was parked in the visitor parking lot, which was way closer than the staff parking lot, ironically enough, given how she had to run if there was an emergency. They walked to her vehicle and he helped her into her SUV. Ava had to blink her eyes to stay awake. These were the times when she hated being a doctor.

The short drive home seemed to take forever.

He didn't drive off, though. From her rearview mirror, she watched him pull up behind her.

"I'm going to warm up some dinner," he said, rushing to catch her at the front door. "And then I'll go check on Balto because I can hear him barking."

"Carson, really. I'm okay."

"You're dead on your feet." He took the keys from

her and she realized she'd been trying to put them in the wrong keyhole. She hadn't bolted the lock.

"Go sit down. I'll get the food ready and then go feed the dog."

"I really just want my bed."

That last word snapped her awake a bit. Why did she get embarrassed by saying it? Silly. He hadn't even noticed. He took off his cowboy hat, hung it on the coat rack before shaking his head. "Sit."

The kitchen smelled heavenly in no time flat, like garlic and thyme and maybe rosemary. He disappeared for a moment, reporting back that Balto was fine, just hungry, and that he'd fed him. So was she, she suddenly realized.

"What are you cooking?"

"My uncle's famous tri-tip, my aunt's green beans and some garlic bread."

Her mouth watered. "I think I could kiss you."

He looked up sharply and the way his eyes narrowed, the way his eyes grew smoky for a split second, made her breath catch. But then he looked away and she could breathe again.

"Eat."

He set the plate down in front of her and she knew that even if her eyes had been closed, she would have sensed his presence. It was as if there were invisible waves that buzzed between them, like the shimmering on a hot road, something that made her forget for a moment that there was food in front of her and that she hadn't eaten in hours and that she was so incredibly tired.

"Bella tells me you forget to eat all the time." He sat opposite her. "No wonder you're so skinny."

She didn't feel skinny. She felt plump and self-conscious and older than her years, especially around a good-looking man like Carson.

"Eat."

She ate. And he was right, she needed food. Ten hours on her feet trying to sew and screw people back together had taken its toll. When she'd nearly finished the first portion, he brought her more then headed to the refrigerator.

"I see you like sweet tea. Do you want some?"He glanced back at her, the door to the refrigerator still open, a questioning look on his face.

"Yes. Please."

She could get used to this, she thought, even though she probably shouldn't think like that, not about him. It wasn't that she didn't want a man in her life. She'd love that. She was just much too sensible to think Carson could fit the bill.

She looked down at her food, the tension returning again, and with it an awareness that she was alone in her house with him. She hadn't been with a man in forever. She missed the warmth and companionship, and Carson was about as good-looking as they came, and she liked him. She might try to keep him at arm's length, but it wasn't because of his personality. He liked her, too. She had a feeling if she were to make one tiny move, a signal to him in ever so slight a way, he'd know what she wanted.

Would he take her up on the silent offer? Did she want him to?

"You feel better now?" he asked, walking back to the table with her drink.

His eyes were so full of concern she wanted to hug him again. This was what she missed—having someone there for her on those days that she could barely drag herself through the front door. Someone looking after her daughter and shouldering the burden so she could take a deep breath. A man to help her forget the stress of her job, one that could remind her that she wasn't just a doctor, but also a woman.

"I can't thank you enough," she said softly.

"You have something there." He pointed to her chin.

"I do?" She wiped where he indicated.

"No, the other side."

She wiped again.

"Here." He got up and his nearness made her as nervous as the day she'd interviewed at Via Del Caballo General. Every muscle in her body went on alert. Her heart rate sped up. She had to force herself not to move.

He used the thumb of his good hand. "You kept missing it." He smiled gently.

This was ridiculous, she told herself. She was a grown woman. She didn't need to melt at his feet, which was about what she felt like doing.

"Thanks."

His hand didn't leave her face. She waited for him to… what? She didn't know. Just waited, the energy between them like a physical tug, an invisible force field that she could feel but not see.

"I really want to kiss you again," he said softly, his thumb swiping the line of her jaw.

Okay, so now was the time to stop. Except…she was too tired to resist. Or maybe she just didn't care, or want to think anymore.

"May I?" he asked.

No. Don't. Big mistake.

She felt herself nod and it was strange because the thought of him kissing her should send her into a panic. Instead it felt absolutely right.

"Come here," he said, reaching out for her.

She felt shy all of a sudden, ducked her head, took a

deep breath. This was it then. The moment when she put everything aside and gave in to her desire. That was all it was. Sexual attraction. She wanted him. He wanted her. She knew what would happen if she stood, told herself that it was okay. They were two adults. She had a right to enjoy a night of passion with a man, even one who was under her care, a good man, someone who clearly cared about not just her, but Bella, too.

She stood.

A crooked little grin spread across his mouth, one that tugged at her heartstrings and made her want to smile. But then he lowered his head and she closed her eyes, and when she felt the first tentative touch of his lips on hers, she sighed.

She wasn't tired anymore.

His hand slipped around her, drew her to him, the pressure of his lips increasing until she did as he silently asked and opened for him. He tasted sweet, like the tea he'd just gulped down. The angle of his head changed and he explored the depths of her mouth even more deeply, his tongue stroking her own in the same rhythm as his hand on her back. Desire gave her the courage to see this thing through. She pressed her palms against his chest, careful not to touch his wounded arm, part of her wondering how they would manage this when he still wore a splint, but then she stopped thinking because the hard contours of his body had her thinking about other things. Damn, he was fit.

He broke off the kiss. She sagged against him.

"Can I take you to bed?"

She throbbed. Her pulse rate escalated all over again. Should she? *Dare* she?

She leaned her head back. It was the look in his eyes

that did it for her. She saw uncertainty there. And hope. And longing. All things she felt, too.

"Yes."

He smiled, bent and kissed her again, then took her hand and led her up the stairs.

Carson had never been more nervous in his life. Not even during the third round of the NFR last year, when he'd been poised to win it all. He'd never felt so out of his depth as he did leading her up the stairs.

"Are you sure about this?" he asked when they paused outside her bedroom door.

Could she really want him? An injured cowboy with a question mark future, who made a tiny fraction of what she did in a year. She answered with a nod and a tiny half smile that made him feel kind of funny inside.

"I'm sure."

So he took his courage into his own hands, told himself he was up to the challenge, leading her into a room that was a mass of contradictions. Frilly where Ava was no-nonsense. Warm where Ava projected an air of cool confidence. Whimsical with its stuffed animals and cartoonlike pieces of artwork on the walls.

She had stopped by the bed and, for such a confident woman, she suddenly seemed awkward, but he knew how she felt. His hands shook he was so nervous.

She had changed earlier, the baggy pink T-shirt she wore making her seem younger. Or maybe it was the trousers. They were baggy and had a striped pattern to them. Hardly sexy attire, but to him she looked adorable.

"This might not be easy," he said, glancing down at his wounded arm.

"How did you get your shirt over it?"

He shot her a wry grin. "Well, it's actually a size

large, and then I looped a rubber band through the buttonhole and then around the button." He held his arm up so she could see.

"Ingenious."

"Desperate to impress you."

He saw her eyes soften at his words, saw the way she licked her lips and yet she also seemed flattered, as if she hadn't expected him to want to try to impress her. If she knew how insecure he felt standing next to her, she'd never doubt his words again.

"Do you have any idea how gorgeous you are?" he asked. "How hard it is to stand here and think, what in the heck does she see in me?"

She dropped her gaze. "You don't have to try and flatter me."

He lifted her chin. "I'm not flattering you. It's true. You're the sexiest woman I've ever met. And if you doubt me, here—" He pulled her hips up against him so she could feel what she did to him.

"No." There was an intensity in her eyes, a sincerity that he couldn't doubt. "If you knew how often I've thought of you over the past few days, you would never say that."

So she felt it, too. That crazy attraction between them. Before he could change his mind, he bent and kissed her again, and it was just like the first time. Exciting. Exhilarating. Unnerving. She tasted like sugar and exotic spices and he could have stood there all night just kissing her. But when she groaned, it did something to him, something that made him want to please her even more. He wanted to impress her, to make her cry out with pleasure, to leave an indelible mark on her that she would never forget.

His hand slipped beneath her shirt, sliding up her rib

cage until he found her nipple. He hated having one hand. Wanted to pick her up and put her on the bed, but he couldn't, so instead he lifted the shirt, pulling his mouth away so he could taste her in another way.

"Carson," she sighed.

Her skin tasted as sweet as her mouth, his tongue swirling around first one hardened nub and then the other. Somehow, maybe he did it, maybe she did, they were at the side of the bed, Ava slipping onto the mattress. Only, he couldn't join her because he'd have to lie on his bad side.

Her gaze met his, her expression puzzled.

"I'm like a chicken with one wing," he said, frustrated with his handicap. He wanted this to be the best night of her life and already he was falling down on the job.

"It's okay," she said with a soft smile. "Lie down."

He drew back in surprise.

She patted next to her on the bed. "Come on. Don't be shy."

Shy? Him? She didn't know him very well, but that didn't mean he liked her taking charge. He wanted to be the one to set the pace, to take charge, to rock her world.

She lifted a brow.

He sat on the edge of the bed. He didn't want to, but he lay down, his good arm bearing the brunt of his weight. Ava scooted over a bit so that she could lean over him, and suddenly she was the master and he was the student.

"I'm going to undress you," she said with a seductive smile. "And then I'm going to do other things to you."

For the first time in his life, a woman took charge and, to his surprise, it sent a charge of arousal through him unlike any he'd felt before. When her hand grazed his zipper, he sighed. When she went from shy schoolgirl to experienced seductress he could barely lie still.

When she unsnapped his pants, then worked the zipper down, he groaned.

Lord, she'd be the death of him.

"Shirt next," she said, leaving his pants open, which was a torture all its own. Her hands made quick work of the buttons on the one arm, and the loops on the other, but she leaned forward to undo his shirt. She smiled at him crookedly as she parted the material, leaning back to stare at him.

"I've been wanting to do this since the first moment I saw you in the exam room." Her hand lifted to his chest, her palm warm, her fingers leaving goose bumps as she followed the curve of his pectorals and then his abdomen.

"You are one naughty doctor," he gasped.

The light in her eyes dulled for a moment and he knew she was thinking about the fact that he was still her patient.

"You're also the sexist woman I've ever seen."

Her rib cage expanded as she stared down at him and then her eyes slid over his body, growing heated, and Carson knew she'd put aside her concerns. He surrendered himself to what she did next, and it was a first for him. Usually he was the one taking the lead. Not tonight.

She gently helped him slip his arm out of his shirt, and he hated that he couldn't do it himself. He couldn't have looked all that great with a black splint on his arm. Granted, she was used to seeing the L-shaped device, but it wasn't like he could reach for her with both arms, which was something he'd really like to do because, for the love of God, he wanted to pull *her* shirt off. Only, he couldn't because—damn it all—he had only one functional arm.

"Better?" she asked with a soft smile when she'd pulled the button-down all the way off.

He smiled wryly. "I can think of something else you could remove that would make it infinitely better."

She cocked a brow at him. It made him want to smile. His professional doctor, alas, not so doctorly tonight. She helped him pull his jeans off and, even with his injury, he could use his left elbow to lift his hips and indicate the black boxer shorts he still wore.

"You match," she said with a smile.

It took him a moment to understand what she meant, mostly because she had driven him close to insanity with the gentle brush of her fingers against his thighs. She meant his black shirt matched his boxers, he realized, closing his eyes because her fingers slipped beneath the waistband of his underwear.

"You're going to be the death of me."

He felt her pull the cotton fabric over his hips and then thighs. And it was so bizarre to simply lie there and do as she bid. It aroused him in a way he'd never experienced before. When she pulled his boxers over his feet and then shifted on the bed, her lips...

"Oh, damn," he groaned because her mouth had found him. He'd never felt so turned on in his life. The feel of her around him did things to his insides he wouldn't have believed possible.

"You're killing me." He gasped.

Where had the prim and proper Dr. Ava Moore learned such things?

Her lips moved away. His eyes popped open because he wanted more, but she was pulling her shirt off, releasing the catches of her bra next so that her pert fullness begged for his attention. He lifted a hand, touched her. She smiled, raising herself on her knees and unsnapping her jeans.

She would go through with it. There was a part of him

that'd wondered if she'd get cold feet, but no. All too soon she was naked over him and tasting him again, and he didn't think he would last if she kept it up.

"Stop." He gasped. "Dear Lord, stop." But he was smiling when he used his good hand to draw her up to him.

"Wait," she said, moving off to the side.

It took him a moment to realize what she was doing, and he found himself surprised that she had protection in her nightstand drawer. She took care of business so quickly that he hardly noticed, picking up right where she'd left off. Thank the Lord for that because he wouldn't have been able to resist if she'd kept it up. It felt too good. And, oddly, it wasn't just the pleasure she gave him that caused him to toss his head back and lose himself in what she did to him, it was the way she controlled everything. He loved that she wasn't shy. That she didn't mind kissing him so intimately, and that as he urged her up, she trailed her mouth along his stomach, her hand taking over where her mouth left off, but not for long. Oh, no. Her fingers fell away and then...

Oh, Lord.

She straddled him and he opened his eyes, Ava staring into his eyes, a soft smile on her face.

"You're killing me," he repeated softly.

"That's the plan."

She moved her hips. He did, too. They found their rhythm quickly, Ava leaning down into him, her mouth finding his, their bodies melding in a whole new way, and he marveled. It was as if she could read his mind. Or perhaps he could read hers. Either way, she seemed to know instinctively how to move, how to change the angle of their union so that he hissed once again, wishing he could flip her beneath him so that he could do the same things to her. He couldn't, though, and rather than fill him with frustration, he let it happen, let himself go.

She broke the kiss, thrust herself away from him and her long hair flicked back. Carson watched as she lost herself to the pleasure of their union. He knew she was close. Their tempo increased, faster and faster until he couldn't keep his bearing any longer. Carson tipped his head back, closing his eyes until light exploded around him and his body flexed and clenched. A spasm of pure pleasure unlike any he'd ever experienced shot through him.

"Ava," he cried out.

She gasped, that was all, and he found it all the more endearing for the way she softly announced her release, her whole body tensing for a moment and then slowly starting to relax.

Her eyes opened.

He hadn't stopped staring at her. He'd enjoyed watching the play of emotion on her face. Her brow had furrowed in concentration and he wondered if she did that during surgery, too. Her mouth had been soft and open and he'd wanted to kiss her, but he had been too transfixed by the sight of her to do more than stare. He watched her slowly come back to him, one corner of her mouth lifting in wry amusement.

"I'd forgotten just how good that feels."

His hand lifted because he couldn't seem to stop himself from touching her face, his fingers sweeping hair off her brow.

"You're remarkable," he whispered.

She lowered her head, rolled off him and onto her side. "I'm not usually so…" Her eyes searched his and she tried to find a word. "Aggressive."

"You were perfect," he said lowly, grateful for the use

of his left arm because he could pull her up to him, rest his chin in her hair. She felt perfect next to him, too. She fit perfect. He rolled onto his side, wishing he had full use of his right arm. He'd hold her tightly. Show her without words how much she meant to him. And the realization caused his heart to race for a whole other reason.

He cared. After his last disastrous relationship with a woman like her, it frightened him to think about how much.

Chapter 13

She slept like she hadn't slept in years. At some point in the wee hours of the morning he must have opened her windows because a breeze blew her drapes into her room, the air causing goose bumps to rise on her skin. Ava pulled the covers closer around her, but they didn't budge.

Carson.

He lay next to her, snoring softly, and she rolled over so she could watch him for a moment. He looked different than when he'd been under anesthesia for surgery. He almost appeared to be smiling, his lips tipped up at the corners, his face relaxed. His five-o'clock shadow had turned into a midnight dusting of hair that made her fingers itch to touch it. He had thick hair, she noticed. It was mussed right now, but it didn't detract from his looks. Paul had had a head of thinning hair. Funny. She'd forgotten about that over the years.

The thoughts of Paul had her turning away. Things had happened quickly with him, too. And though she tried not to compare the two, it was hard not to do exactly that. She'd often wondered what would have happened if she'd forced herself to slow down where Paul was concerned. She'd fallen so hard and so fast she hadn't thought about the consequences of loving a man who constantly put his life in danger. Carson didn't like to climb cliffs, though. Riding was still dangerous, sure. Her heart had been in her throat while watching Bella ride, but it wasn't like he rode wild broncs. It was other things that worried her. His time on the road. The women who would chase him. Her own fears of inadequacy that might lead to trouble down the road.

But she was getting ahead of herself. One night did not a relationship make. Right now she needed to check on her patients, something she'd have to do before she went to pick up Bella. Hopefully she could make her rounds quickly and pick Bella up from the ranch midmorning. She'd text her daughter to have the Gillians call her if there were any problems, but they seemed happy to watch her. And she should check on Balto, too. He was probably tired of being in that kennel...all of which meant she needed to get out of bed.

For some reason, she didn't want to wake Carson, so she quietly padded down the hall to use Bella's shower. She told herself it was because she didn't need to bother him, but she'd always prided herself on being honest with herself. Her thoughts of Paul and the comparisons to Carson had her on edge as she silently went about the house and got ready for the day. Still, she couldn't just leave him, and so before she left the house she quickly scribbled him a note telling him she'd see him later at the ranch. Hopefully she'd pull it together by then.

She lost herself in her work at the hospital that morning. It was the one thing she could always count upon, her passion for what she did for a living.

"Wow. What happened to you?"

Ava straightened from the chart she'd been studying. "What do you mean?"

Nurse Bell studied her face. "You're glowing."

That gave her pause, but only for a moment. "I'm pleased

with my patients' progress," she admitted. "They're all stable with no sign of infection."

Nurse Bell nodded. "I heard about your emergency surgery last night. Damn drunk drivers." The young nurse shook her head. "Carson Gillian called for you earlier, by the way. Left a message at reception."

Carson.

She shouldn't be surprised he'd called. She'd been avoiding her cell phone all morning.

"Thanks."

Sure enough, she had a missed call from Carson on her cell. Nothing from Bella or the rest of the Gillians, though, and that was good. Her daughter appeared to have found some new friends. She debated with herself on whether or not to call him back, but she wasn't fifteen years old. She was a mature adult who was perfectly capable of conversing with a man she'd spent most of the night kissing.

She dialed him on her cell.

"Doctor, help," said a deep masculine voice when the line connected. "I think I might need a house call."

She smiled. "You're incorrigible."

He didn't say anything. She looked around the employee lounge, almost as if someone might have overheard him, which she knew was ridiculous, but she couldn't help but feel self-conscious. For one, she could get into trouble if anyone found out about them. Not terrible trouble, but she was new to Via Del Caballo General, too new to break unspoken rules.

"I missed you this morning." She heard him take a deep breath. "And I have to tell you, that's not like me. I'm usually the one that wakes up and takes off."

She wasn't sure how to take the comment. It inferred

waking up in someone else's bed was nothing new for him, whereas she hadn't been with anyone since Paul.

"Not that I'm constantly in bed with women." His words were laced with embarrassment.

"Well, I should hope not."

"I'm not the one that calls the next morning, either."

Her brow creased, not that he could see it.

"Which makes me sound even more like a player," he admitted with obvious distress. "You know what? I'm just going to shut the hell up and tell you that I missed you this morning and I'm glad I get to see you at some point today. Bella's having a great time here. I have her busy mucking stalls and exercising horses. She'll probably sleep like a baby tonight." He paused then added, "That's all I wanted to say."

It was a moment when she could offer a pithy comment back or take the first tentative step toward something deeper.

"I missed you, too," she admitted.

She heard him release a breath, had a feeling he smiled on the other end. "Good."

She didn't want to say too much. This was all too new. *Too terrifying.*

"So, dinner tonight?" he asked.

And this was another one of those moments. "Carson, can we just slow down a little bit? I don't want to…" She looked down at the tile floor beneath her feet. "Rush into anything."

"You mean you don't want to spend every waking moment with me?"

He tried to make a joke of it, she could tell by the tone of his words, but it fell flat.

"I want a full night of sleep," she said, hoping he

wouldn't take the words as a brush-off. "Emergency surgeries take a physical toll on me and combined with…"

"Hot, steamy sex," he finished for her.

She huffed despite herself. "Yes, that. I'm just exhausted. What I need right now is a nap."

"Okay then. I can understand that."

"Good."

"I'll see you when you get here."

But as she hung up the phone she wondered what she would have done if picking up Bella wasn't necessary. The thought of facing him after what they'd done made her flush. Would she have taken a short break? Given them a few days to get their thoughts in order? To figure out where the hell this was going? Alas, she didn't have a choice.

The best laid plans…

Carson checked his cell phone once again before tucking it back in his pocket and returning his attention to Bella, who was pulling on Snazzy's reins. No new messages. Well, aside from the one she'd sent him just before he'd helped Bella mount Snazzy.

Called into surgery again. Going to be late. Do you mind keeping Bella a bit longer?

"She's not coming, is she?" Bella asked, guiding Snazzy back to him. She shook her head, lower lip thrust out before she said, "I hate when this happens."

"It's for a good reason." But he understood how she felt. Life with Ava would always be a guessing game.

The thought gave him pause.

It implied a potential, as if he was thinking about a

future with Ava. But that was ridiculous. They'd really just met.

"You're probably lucky you saw her last night," Bella grumbled.

He'd told Bella he'd made sure his mom had made it home safely last night. That was all she knew. She'd tried to ask more questions, but Carson had brushed her off, telling her they ought to focus on her riding while she was staying at the ranch. She'd been only too happy to comply. The last thing he needed was for Bella to catch wind of what was going on between him and her mother. He had a feeling Ava would lose her mind if something slipped out, not that he'd blame her. Bella was too young.

"Why don't you unsaddle Snazzy and I'll take you up to my dad's house. I know you've been dying to see our collection of rodeo stuff."

His dad had been off delivering horses last night when his uncle had told Bella all about their rodeo memorabilia. She'd begged him to see it this morning.

"That'd be so cool." She slipped off Snazzy, patting her before throwing the reins over her head and leading her out of the arena. "I had so much fun with your family last night, Carson. They're really great."

He had to admit they really were. Of course, they'd all been curious about the little girl he'd brought to the ranch. His sister might have lectured him on the pros and cons of dating a woman with a child, but the rest of the family had teased him about having a crush. Carson had denied there was anything to it, but deep down inside he knew they were right. Which left him where, exactly? he wondered. He had a thing for Ava, no doubt. But long-term? He didn't think anything could come of it. They were just too different. She wanted to save the world. He wanted to win a world championship. A woman with a kid was not part of the plan, even if he did adore Ava's child.

"Are you excited about the horse show next weekend?" he asked as he gingerly took off Snazzy's saddle. He sent Ava a text message about where they'd be, not surprised when all he received back was a thumbs-up icon.

Bella's face lit up. "I can't wait." But then it fell again. "I just hope my mom can take me."

They were just going to watch. And the show he had in mind was only two hours away. Surely she could take a day trip every now and again. He should probably talk to her about it, though, express how much Bella looked forward to going. At some point she had to put aside being a doctor for her daughter's sake. There were a lot of things he should probably discuss with her, such as pretending as if last night had never happened. Maybe that would be for the best.

The sound of the metal snaps hitting the stall walls brought him back to the present. Bella was leading Snazzy into her stall.

"Maybe I'll talk with her today." But he wasn't talking about the horse show. Bella smiled in excitement and he felt bad for a moment. The kid clearly had her hopes up that things would work out between him and her mom. Little did she know.

"Did something happen with you and my mom last night, Carson?"

He almost tripped. What the heck had made her think that? And what did a nine-year-old know about what happened between a man and a woman? Hell's bells, that was not a question he wanted to know the answer to.

So he hedged as he led Bella to the Gator they would use to drive up to his dad's house. "She was tired. I made sure she got home safe. I made sure she ate, too, as per your own orders."

The sideways look the little girl shot him made him want to slink into the ATV seat. He aimed the Gator toward the gravel road that led to the top of a small hill and to his dad's house. His aunt and uncle's home sparkled in the distance on the next hill over.

"Do you think you might become her boyfriend?"

He weighed his words carefully. "I think I'd like to be her friend first."

The words seemed to satisfy the little girl and he was grateful to let the matter drop. Conversations with a nine-year-old were not his forte.

"Every time we come up here, I think how pretty it is."

Carson's eyes focused on the house in front of them. "It's home," he offered. "Well, not anymore. I live in a bunkhouse with Flynn and Maverick and a cousin now."

"Your dad's place reminds me of a Spanish hotel. Kind of like the barn."

He supposed it did look like one, although much smaller. The single-story home had a Spanish tiled roof and stucco sides that matched the barn. Behind it, there was a sweeping view of the valley below. Inside, the Spanish theme continued with terra-cotta floors and dark beams overhead.

"Oh, wow," she said when she went inside.

"Anyone home?" Carson called.

"Back here," answered his dad.

"This is amazing." Bella had stopped in the entryway, in front of a wall of NFR back numbers and a few of the saddles that came along with winning a world championship. Over the years his family had won many—especially his dad and uncle Bob, who'd competed in team roping back in the day. "Look. One of them has your name on it. Is that the one you wore at the NFR last year?"

"You know I went to the NFR?"

"I read about you on the internet." She glanced up at him. "Actually before we met."

"You're kidding?"

She nodded proudly. "When my mom told me we'd be visiting your ranch I knew exactly who you were."

"I'll be darned."

"You're going back this year, right?" she asked.

"If the arm's okay."

And what then? He was crazy if he thought he could fit Ava and Bella into his life.

"It will be," Bella said, confidence on her young face. "My mom fixed it for you."

And then it would be back to the grind. Working horses for his dad and hitting the rodeo circuit when he could. Except…

As he stared at those numbers he realized how scared he was. And it was funny because before his accident he would have told anyone who'd asked that making it to the NFR was no big deal. He'd always held the belief that if it happened, it happened. But then he'd faced a possible career-ending injury, one that would force him to give lessons to little girls like Bella for the rest of his life—that and build furniture—and he didn't like that idea. Not one bit. Sure, he enjoyed it and took pride in it, but he didn't want that to be his whole life. He'd realized that he didn't want to look back and regret that he hadn't done something more.

"Come on." He waved her toward the back of the house. "I'll introduce you to my dad. He's the one with most of the numbers up there on the wall. He and my uncle were pretty famous back in the day."

She smiled excitedly and, man, he really liked having Bella around. Her enthusiasm for horseback riding was contagious. It made him think of his younger days, back when he'd wanted nothing more than to spend the whole day in the barn. He'd lost some of that joy in recent years. Bella helped to rekindle his youthful enthusiasm.

"There he is," said a voice from inside his dad's office as they entered the room.

"Shane," Carson said, clapping his brother on the shoulder with his good hand. "When'd you get back into town?" His brother had flown home to North Carolina after his surgery.

"Last night." Shane drew back, turning to his wife. "We had to rush back to approve the plans with Dad for the new house." His gaze dropped to Carson's splint. "How's the elbow?"

"Good." He lifted it to show Shane his incisions. "Better. I'm supposed to get this off next week."

"I bet that will feel better."

Carson pulled Shane's beautiful wife, Kait, into his arms next—well, one of his arms, the good one—leering down at her for the benefit of his brother. It was all in good fun.

"How's my pretty sister-in law?" he asked.

"Glad to be back in California."

Shane's wife was a famous race-car driver, her blond hair and blue eyes recognizable to race fans around the world. It seemed like an odd match for her to hook up with his bull-rider brother, but the two of them made it work. These days they were busy raising twins, something that would test a lot of marriages but hadn't seemed to faze the couple.

"Where's my newest niece and nephew?" Carson asked, looking around.

"Over at your aunt and uncle's place," said Kait. "I don't know what I'd do without Aunt Crystal."

His aunt seemed to be everyone's go-to babysitter, including Jayden's. His aunt would frequently make the trek to his sister's apartment to watch Paisley when Jayden had to go to class.

"Everyone, this is Bella, the young lady I'm giving horseback riding lessons to as a favor for her mom. Dad, Bella wanted to meet the man with all the numbers on the wall."

Reese Gillian stood, his knees popping in a way that reminded Carson his dad was getting old. Beneath a tan-colored felt hat, his dad's eyes studied their young guest. Bella moved closer to his side, as if Reese Gillian intimidated her and she sought out his reassurance.

"Nice to meet you, young lady."

Bella stared up at him in awe. "I read on the internet that you hold the record for the most average wins at the NFR."

His dad nodded and he even smiled a little at the girl, and Carson marveled. Ever since he'd had heart surgery he'd been a different man, more easygoing and laid back. Last year he'd have probably grunted a one-word response. Today he hooked his thumbs in his jeans pockets and said, "Yup. Me and Carson's uncle."

"That's cool." She looked up at Carson. "I can't wait to watch Carson compete at the NFR."

"Pffft," Shane snorted. "You might have a long wait time."

Bella frowned. "What do you mean?"

"Carson doesn't believe in setting goals. He prefers to let things sort of happen. He spent two years loafing around before he made it to the NFR, something that didn't seem to bother him. With that kind of drive to succeed, he'll be too old to compete by the time he makes it back."

Despite the grin on Shane's face, it was criticism he deserved. A year ago he would even have agreed with his brother. Not anymore.

"Too old?" Carson shook his head. "Give me a break. I'll outlast you and your bull riding, that's for sure. And once my arm is healed, I'll be hitting the rodeo trail hard."

"My mom fixed it for him," Bella said with pride.

"He's lucky to have her," Reese said.

"You want to see the house we're going to build?" Kait asked Bella.

"Yes!" Bella said excitedly.

They all shuffled over to Reese's desk, where a beam of light from outside spotlighted the plans. It was an elevated drawing of a single-story home. No frills. Nothing fancy. Just a cute little ranch home with dormers across the front—nothing like what Carson had in mind for a home. He wanted a Colonial revival type with a half-round porch across the front and a hip-and-valley roof with wide columns across the front holding it up.

That won't happen if you don't make it to the NFR.

"That's really pretty," Bella observed.

Not as pretty as what he would build.

Shane must have known what Carson was thinking. "It doesn't need to be fancy. We'll only be around part of the time. Besides, you should see Kait's house in North Carolina."

"No. It's great," Carson said.

"What do you think could be better?"

He picked up the blueprints and lost himself to reviewing the plans. Bella asked if she could go explore the house, and she went off for a tour with Kait. He hardly noticed her absence as he sat across from his father, who returned to his other duties, while Carson dedicated himself to something he loved. When he heard a car drive up, he realized it was Ava. Finally back from the hospital. *Bella must feel like an orphan sometimes.*

"Who's that?" Reese asked.

"That's Bella's mom."

His dad grunted. That was more like him.

A moment later they heard a knock, knock.

Then the sound of small feet padding quickly down the hall. "Mom!" Bella cried. "Look at these saddles. Aren't they cool?"

"I'll go greet her," Carson said, his stomach suddenly tight as it was on the morning of a competition.

Shane caught him on his way out of the office, though. "Mighty nice of you to give the kid lessons."

He frowned. "It's not like that."

His brother leaned back. "Sure it's not."

Chapter 14

It was like arriving for biology lab a half hour late. Ava wanted to snatch Bella and run right back out.

"You're here," Bella said, slinking into her arms. Ava felt a twinge of guilt for staying away for so long.

"I am," she said, bending to hug her daughter while surreptitiously looking for Carson. He wasn't around.

"Isn't this place neat?"

"It is." Carson had texted her earlier that they were up at the big house, and to let herself in.

She took in her surroundings. Dark beams came together above their heads, like hands in a steeple, the fingers holding up the roof to protect them. They stood in the foyer that opened into a massive family room with terra-cotta floors. On every surface were buckles and Western bric-a-brac and she realized they were trophies. A hand-painted box with a brass plaque on the front and the name of what she surmised was a horse show etched into the metal. A pair of chaps hung in one corner. In front of a leather-and-cowhide couch sat a coffee table with a glass surface. Beneath, the rope lighting around the border of the table illuminated buckles. National Finals Rodeo was printed on all of them, sometimes the name big and bold, other times, on the older buckles, smaller but no less stunning. The assortment of dates was impressive.

"Look at how many buckles there are," Bella said, turning in place. "I wonder how many Carson has won."

"Not as many as everyone else."

Carson.

He came at her from down a hall that ran the length of the house to her left and right, and there it was again, the tingling sensation that tickled her belly and warmed her cheeks. Why did he always have to look so handsome? Today he wore a white long-sleeved button-down and his black cowboy hat.

"At least he admits what a slacker he is," said someone else behind him—a tall man with thick sideburns and a face so much like Carson's. She remembered him from the hospital as one of Carson's brothers.

"Dr. Moore, you remember my brother Shane? And this is his wife, Kait." He pointed to a gorgeous blonde who seemed faintly familiar to Ava for some reason. "You've met my dad, Reese Gillian."

Dr. Moore? She supposed she should be glad he sounded so formal.

"Nice to see you all."

"What do you mean Carson is a slacker?" Bella asked.

Shane smiled ruefully. "Carson's a born team roper. He has the talent to be one of the best in the business, just not the drive. And now with his elbow on the fritz…"

He wasn't serious about competing? Why did that take her by surprise?

"His elbow will be fine," Ava said firmly. "There's no reason why he can't go back to roping again."

"I'm glad to hear that," said his dad.

"I'll make sure he goes to the NFR," Bella said with a nod of her head. "He'll do what I ask him to do."

Ava smiled at her daughter's simplistic outlook on life.

"Things come too easy to him," Reese said. "Riding. Roping. Women. He's never had to actually work at something."

Women? Right. Not that she needed the reminder.

"I'm standing right here, Dad."

"I know, I know." His dad shushed him with a hand. "Maybe the good doctor will light a fire under your butt because I wish, for once in your life, you'd focus on something you're good at."

"I'm good at making furniture and I've showed how well I can focus there."

"That's a hobby. Are you saying you'd walk away from the rodeo for that?"

"No, I'm not." Carson's eyes gleamed.

Ava stared between him and his dad, her stomach suddenly dropping for reasons she didn't understand. There was a glint in his eyes, an almost feverish intensity that reminded her of Paul.

"As soon as my arm is better, I'm hitting the rodeo trail." His gaze encircled the room. "Hard. Nothing's going to get in the way of me making it to the NFR. Nothing."

Nothing? Was he looking at her?

"Well, first things first. We'll see if your elbow heals correctly and that will determine when and if you can ride again."

"You said it'd be fine and it will be."

Just like Paul in so many ways. He'd injured his hand a week before he'd died. She'd told him not to go. He'd done it anyway.

Ava looked away. It wasn't like Carson would die if he fell off a horse. It shouldn't upset her that he seemed so determined to make it to the NFR, but it did for some reason and it suddenly occurred to her why. It wasn't just that he'd go off and leave them both, it was that he'd do it even if it was against her wishes and her medical advice. She could see it in his eyes. She couldn't go through that again. And how many times had she vowed that the next man she dated would be a homebody? Someone who put her and her daughter's needs first. And here she was, the first man she'd taken an interest in since Paul, and he was exactly like him.

How could she make the same mistake twice?

Chapter 15

Something had happened.

Carson couldn't quite put his finger on it, but Ava had seemed pensive when she'd said her goodbyes. He wondered if he should call her later, but something in her eyes had told him to give her a little space. Slow down, like she'd asked.

He waited to text her until the next day. Her reply was terse, something about a busy week and that she'd see him at his follow-up appointment on Wednesday.

He read and then re-read the message over and over again. Brush-off. All that talk about him being a cowboy and going to the NFR must have reminded her of who he really was. Blue collar. A man who made his living off the back of his horse. Not her type. He should have figured.

The day of his appointment he drove to the hospital, feeling as jittery as their barn cat, Duke, whenever one of the cattle dogs was around. Maybe he should try to talk to her if they had a moment alone. But the thought of doing so opened up a pit in the bottom of his stomach. She'd made it clear she didn't want anything further to do with him. He was her daughter's riding instructor. That was all. Although maybe she wanted to stop even that.

Not surprisingly he became even more jittery while he sat in a sterile all-white exam room, the paper on the exam table crinkling beneath his butt. He'd already had an X-ray. His arm looked weird without the brace on it. Felt funny, too. Lighter somehow. So he sat there, tense, staring at the scars above his elbow, worried about his future yet perversely excited to see Ava again.

"Mr. Gillian," she said, bursting into the room so suddenly his heart leaped. "Good to see you again."

Yup. She was done with him. He could tell by the way she wouldn't make eye contact.

It stung.

"Let's take a look at that arm," she said, setting down her tablet.

He was about to ask her what was wrong but then he saw a nurse come in behind her. He held his tongue.

Her grip was light, yet firm, and Carson thought she couldn't look more buttoned-up if she'd tried. She wore a starched collared white shirt beneath her white coat, her hair pulled back off her head, minimal makeup, no jewelry. It was like working with a stranger. The fingers that'd caressed him so softly over the weekend were now coolly professional as she turned his elbow this way and that. She acted like they'd never met.

"Looks good," she said, releasing him and stepping back. She even stuffed her hands in her damn pockets. "I've already reviewed the X-rays. Your bones have knitted together perfectly. I don't see any reason why you couldn't start physical therapy later this week, which means your primary care physician will be taking over from me for now. There'll be a follow-up visit with me in a few weeks, just to make sure your therapy is working, but we should be good. I'll have the therapist go easy on you at first, then increase the load." She picked up her tablet, wrote something down, the quintessential doctor, and it left him sitting there with his mouth slightly open.

"You're still a ways away from riding a horse, but you're on the right track."

It was like she didn't even know him.

"Can I talk to you alone?" he asked softly, hoping the nurse wouldn't hear. He stared at her so intently that he saw the way her pupils flared, the way her lips pressed together.

"What about?" she said.

"It's personal," he answered.

Her eyes narrowed. She knew exactly what "personal" matter he wanted to speak to her about. Clearly she didn't want to do as he asked, but she tipped her head toward the nurse. "Can you give us a moment please?"

"Of course," said the petite blonde.

The nurse slipped out the door at the same time Ava reached for her tablet again, this time holding it in front of her like a shield. She pasted a politely professional smile on her face.

"What's up?"

Never before had he been on the receiving end of a brush-off. To be honest, he didn't like it. Not one bit.

"Why have you shut me down?"

"What do you mean?"

Man, there were times when she frustrated the heck out of him. "Look, I may not be as smart as you, but I can tell you regret what happened between us. Either that or my dad said something to upset you. Was it all that talk about being a cowboy?"

"What are you talking about?" She seemed genuinely perplexed.

He reached out to her with his good arm, forgetting for a moment that he no longer had his splint and that he could have used his other hand, but in the end it didn't matter. She took a step back before their flesh could connect.

"Is it that I'm not good enough for you?"

Her face registered surprise. "Carson, that's not it at all."

Did she mean it? He searched her eyes, trying to glean the truth, but it was like looking for the answer in a sky full of stars.

"All right, what is it then?"

She stared down at the floor for a moment while she seemed to collect her thoughts. Carson's heart began to pound. He felt like he had the one time he'd ridden a bull. The one and only time.

"I just don't think this is a good idea."

"What do you mean by 'this'?"

She shook her head. "Look. I'm sorry." She still held that damn tablet in front of her, knuckles blanched, she clutched it so hard. "I'm not used to jumping into bed with someone. I feel out of my depth. I need time to sort it all out. And then there's Bella to think about, too, and she's already grilling me about what happened. I just think it's better if we cool it for a little while."

"Cool it? Or end it?"

He saw her take a deep breath, saw her eyes fill with something like sadness. "I'm not sure."

The words gave him hope but the look in her eyes did not. "What about lessons? You want to continue with those?"

"Of course."

"And what about the show this weekend? You're still bringing Bella? You know how much she's looking forward to it."

"Of course we're still going. Bella can't stop talking about it. We'll just keep it cool between us, okay? For

Bella's sake. I don't want her to think I don't like you or something."

Keep it cool. Yeah, right. He had a feeling she'd "keep it cool" right up until the moment she dumped him.

She scooted toward the exit. "I'll write up an order for your PT. My nurse will find you a brace you can wear in the meantime, something you can use if your arm gets sore. I'll have her make that follow-up visit for you, too."

She opened the door. "Nice to see you again, Mr. Gillian. Thank you for everything you're doing for my daughter."

She was gone.

He left her alone.

Ava was grateful for that. It allowed her to focus on what she did best—being a doctor. And while she wasn't exactly looking forward to dealing with Carson at the horse show, she did look forward to a few days off work. Bella had been insistent that they make a weekend of it, and if she were honest, Ava felt a little guilty for being so busy lately, so she'd taken some time off. The hotel where they were staying looked more like a Mexican resort, from the photos she'd seen online. She planned to have some fun with Bella while they were out of town.

So she found herself driving through the desert a few days later, toward a resort town that they could barely make out in the distance. Outside, scrub and cactus and piles of rock dotted the landscape on either side. They drove down a little two-lane highway, grateful for the air-conditioning inside.

"Do you think Carson would let me show a horse this weekend if I ask?"

Ava smiled ruefully, shaking her head. "I think that might be a bit of a long shot, honey, but you never know."

Carson.

Damn that man. She'd been trying to push him from her mind all week, to think things through. She refused to rush into something like she had with Paul. This weekend it might be hard to keep him at a distance. Seeing him in her exam room had only driven home the one thing she couldn't deny—she was still attracted to him. If only he were a different kind of man.

"There's no way I'm going to be able to sleep tonight," Bella gushed with a slap-happy grin that warmed Ava's heart. That was what she needed to do. Focus on the positives. Despite the disaster that she'd made of her relationship with Carson, at least she couldn't fault her decision to let Bella have riding lessons. She'd never seen her so happy. "I've always wanted to go to a horse show. Carson said the class he wants me to watch is first thing in the morning."

Which meant with any luck they'd get in, get out and be off. She could keep the Carson time down to a minimum.

"Do you think we could go to the show grounds tonight? I'd like to see everyone before they show tomorrow."

Ava's stomach dropped. "I'm not sure, honey. You'll have to ask Carson."

Please don't ask. Please. Please.

She should have known better. Bella's little fingers went to work on her cell phone while Ava tried to concentrate on the road. But it was useless. She had way too much time to think. So she let her mind free of its corral. She felt terrible about keeping Carson at arm's length. But that didn't mean she should let her guard down. She would not jump into bed again, not until they'd both had some time to think. She'd done her best to keep her distance, but she couldn't escape the notion that she might have handled things badly. She could admit that. She felt guilty, and anxious, too, because she'd be seeing him soon and she didn't want things to be awkward between them.

Bing.

She tensed. That had to be Carson replying to Bella's text.

Her daughter's face lit up. "He said we could come by the show grounds, and that I could even ride tonight to help the horses practice if I wanted to," Bella all but squealed.

Ava winced inwardly because that meant she'd be seeing the man sooner rather than later. But maybe that was for the best. Get it out of the way so she wouldn't be stressing about it all night long.

"What are you typing?" she asked Bella, who was furiously tapping at her screen.

"He asked when we'd be arriving."

"What'd you tell him?"

"That we were almost there."

Oh, dear goodness. That meant seeing him *really* soon, she thought, checking her appearance in the mirror. Why hadn't she left her hair down and put some makeup on this morning?

Why do you care?

She refused to answer the question.

"Oh, wow, Mom…is that the place?"

She'd been so deep in thought she hadn't been paying attention to her surroundings, just following the directions given to her by her GPS device. They were on the outskirts of Palm Springs, in a belt of green she wouldn't have thought possible this far into the desert. Off in the distance, the equestrian center stood out like a miniature city, the red-metal roof of what she supposed was a massive covered arena catching the rays of the sun.

In no time they were there and Ava was pulling up in front of the place. What looked like horse stalls, only made out of some kind of plastic, stood on either side of the main facility. People came and went, most of them leading a horse to the arena, a few walking, some in golf carts. The stalls looked like they went on and on.

"Look at that huuuge cactus," Bella said, eyes wide, her face in profile as she stared out the window at the large succulent. "Can I go see it up close?"

Ava checked her mirrors for horses and more cars pulling in. "Sure. Just be sure to walk. We don't want you scaring any horses."

"I know, *Mom*." She didn't quite roll her eyes but it was close. "Be right back."

And she was off, Ava smiling despite herself. She didn't blame Bella for being intrigued. She wanted to check out the huge saguaro, too. She'd only ever seen them in movies and pictures, and they were way bigger than she expected. She grabbed her keys and purse before taking a deep breath. Time to face the music, she thought, her mood plummeting again. But it was good to get this out of the way. She wouldn't have to spend a sleepless night dreading seeing Carson in person. She slipped out of her SUV and into the warm desert air.

And came face-to-face with the man himself.

Chapter 16

He'd surprised her.

"Hello," he said awkwardly.

She forced a smile. He did, too. They were like two chess players facing off at the end of a game.

"Hi," she said softly.

Damn, she looked beautiful. She'd worn a loose-fitting shirt, one the same shade of green as her eyes. She'd pulled her hair back, too, but not in a ponytail. It loosely framed her face, wide hoop earrings catching the light of the sun.

"I figured it would be easier if I showed you where we were stalled rather than you wandering around."

He didn't want her thinking he was trying to see her when she'd made it clear she wanted space. It was a big place. Impossible to text directions…or so he told himself.

Bella came running up. "Carson," she cried, arms outstretched, and Carson did something that came totally naturally. He pulled her into a hug.

"There she is," he said with a tug on her hair and a teasing smile. "Are you excited about watching the horse show this weekend?"

She nodded enthusiastically. "I can't wait."

"You don't have to stick around," he told Ava.

He could have sworn she stood straighter. "No. That's okay. I'd like to watch her ride."

"Good thing I'm wearing my boots," Bella said, lifting

her pants and exposing the boots they'd bought… Was that only two weeks ago? It seemed like forever.

"Where do we go?" Bella looked at the stalls around them.

"Actually we're inside. Come on. I'll show you where our barn is."

He led them to an entrance off to the side of the arena. Inside, dozens of riders were putting their horses through their paces. His dad was in there somewhere. The show was over for the day, but everyone needed to practice for tomorrow. That was when the real action would start. There would be all kinds of classes throughout the weekend— from open cutting to futurities for the younger horses—all to show off the horses and their training in front of judges who would determine who was the best of the lot.

Carson nodded at a few of the riders as they passed by, leading Ava and Bella through the main portion of the arena and into a second section, one with double rows of stalls facing each other. Some of the corner stalls had canvas covers on them in red, or green or gray, the colors varied—barn colors. The name of the training stable denoted which group of stalls belonged to the colors.

"Oh, Mom, look. They decorated."

"Everyone does that," he clarified. "It's kind of a thing."

Brown drapes hung along the front of their own place. A sign with an iron cutout of their brand hung on a wall, beneath which sat a couch. An actual leather couch that his dad insisted on taking to each show. Carson didn't mind. He'd made the thing and it brought in more business than he cared to admit, no matter how silly he thought it was to dress up a horse stall.

"This is neat."

The words had him looking around as if seeing it for the first time. There were other stall fronts more elaborately decorated than theirs. Some had director's chairs out front, people sitting around relaxing and chatting; others had even gone to the trouble of putting down indoor/outdoor carpeting; one had a white picket fence around the front. He supposed it would look pretty cool to an outsider, especially one as horse crazy as Bella. Her mom, however, seemed unimpressed. That didn't surprise him.

"So I had an idea." Carson stopped in front of their own group of stalls. "Actually it was my dad's idea. One of the reasons why I had you riding Snazzy is that we're trying to sell her as a youth horse. My dad thought it was great that you're doing so well, so we were thinking it'd be great advertising if Bella showed her in a cutting class tomorrow."

Silence. Bella's mouth dropped open just before she screeched, *"What!"* so loudly that everyone around them turned to look.

"Bella," her mom chastised.

"Oh my gosh. Mom, pleeezzz. Can I? Can I please?" She clutched her hands together and for the first time in days Carson felt like smiling. "We were just talking about that on the way here but my mom said it would never happen, me showing that is, but now here you are and, oh, Mom, can I please?"

"I never said it wouldn't happen."

Ava clearly didn't like being put on the spot. He tried not to feel sorry for her. Actually he tried not to feel a lot of things for her as he stared down at her. She'd hurt him with her standoffish behavior. He didn't like the way it turned his insides out.

"Won't Snazzy be…I don't know, different to ride at a horse show?" Ava's eyes reflected her concern. "More hyper or something?"

Carson rubbed his elbow, something he didn't even

realize he'd been doing until he followed the direction of her gaze. It'd been hurting a bit, probably because of the PT he'd been doing. Plus he'd been working it a little too hard helping his dad get ready for the show this week. She was probably thinking he should be wearing his brace.

"Actually I think she could do it. Those two days in a row she spent with us really tightened her legs. She'll be able to hold on."

"Oh, Mom, can I?"

Ava stared at her daughter, her eyes full of concern. "Why don't we see how it goes today and then we can decide?"

"Fair enough." Carson turned away. "Bella, come help me get Snazzy ready."

He tried to ignore Ava as they set about saddling up the horse. He'd liked Ava. Seeing her again only brought that home. Sure, he had no idea if a relationship with her would work out in the end, but he would have liked a shot at it. Or maybe not. He had to admit her behavior these past few days had lit a fire in his belly to make it to the NFR. She claimed the fact that he was a cowboy wasn't an issue, but there was a part of him that didn't believe her. He had to show her that he was her equal in every way.

"You ready?" he asked Bella.

"I think I might be sick."

"Just take it easy," Ava advised.

"Snazzy knows you," Carson added. "She'll take care of you. That's why she's such a great youth horse."

"Maybe we could buy her, Mom."

Ava's gaze flicked in his direction. "Maybe."

Not if she knew Snazzy's price tag, Carson thought. He was tempted to tell her just to watch her face fill with shock. She probably had no clue how much show horses were worth. And rope horses, too. He'd been offered a small fortune for Rooster. He'd never sell him, though, especially not now.

"Just go on in and warm her up," Carson said, opening the arena gate for Bella.

"Are you sure she shouldn't…I don't know, use a different arena? One that's less crowded."

He could tell Ava was growing more and more nervous at the prospect of Bella showing. "She'll be fine."

"Yeah, but won't she be required to chase a cow or something in the competition? Isn't that what cutting is? She's never worked with live cattle before. If she falls off she might get trampled."

"She won't fall off."

He hadn't been kidding about Bella's ability to ride. She'd impressed the hell out of him when he'd had her ride some of his dad's horses. Even his brother Flynn had come down to watch, commenting on her ability.

"She looks good."

His dad had come up on the rail, stopping his favorite and more famous cutting horse, a sorrel they called Rooster because of his quick moves.

"I think she'll be fine," Reese said in a tone of confident optimism.

"I think so, too, Dad."

Ava didn't say anything, although she'd waved a greeting when his dad trotted up. They all watched Bella kick Snazzy into a canter, meshing with the people on the rail like an old pro.

"You got clothes for her to show in? She'll need a nice button-down and a cowboy hat," Reese said.

"She brought her cowboy hat. It's in the car. I don't know about a shirt, though."

"There's a mobile tack store out back," Reese said. "Put whatever she needs on my account."

"Oh, no. I couldn't do that."

"It's my pleasure," his dad said. "You're doing me a favor. Bet we'll have her sold by the end of the show once word gets out a rookie who's ridden less than half a dozen times is out there working cows."

His dad tipped his hat at Ava before riding off again, the gesture old-school but not surprising coming from his dad. Carson watched as Reese rode up alongside Ava. He was clearly giving her instructions, the two of them riding to the center of the arena a bit later. Carson knew what his dad wanted Bella to do.

"Watch this," he told Ava.

"Watch what?"

In the middle of the arena, Bella turned Snazzy around sharply, the horse's hind end staying in place, the first turn slow, the second one faster, the third one so quick Bella had to clutch the horn. Ava gasped.

The mare stopped.

Bella laughed, her giggle flying across the arena and landing on Carson's heart. Nothing like a kid on a horse to lift a man's spirits.

Bella pulled on the reins, spinning in the other direction.

"I don't think I can watch this." Ava turned her back to them. "I don't think she's ready. She almost fell off."

"Relax. She won't be spinning in a cutting class. Dad's just showing her Snazzy's moves, and probably assessing her ability to hold on. If she'd come off, he'd have nixed the idea of her riding tomorrow."

"I mean it, Carson. I don't think I can let her do this. I need more time to get used to the idea of Bella doing something dangerous."

Like she'd needed more time for them? He almost asked the question but decided against it. "If my dad says she's good to go, you can bet she'll be just fine. I think she can do it, too."

"You're not Bella's father."

No. Bella's father was dead. The words hung in the air between then, Carson suddenly realizing where her fear came from. She'd lost one person to a tragic accident. She was terrified of it happening again.

"I would never let anything happen to her. You have to know that."

"Horses are unpredictable. You can't always control what they're going to do. I'm not prepared to take the risk."

Was that why she'd let things cool between them, too? Was she worried that if she cared for him too much he might get hurt…like Paul. It seemed a completely crazy idea, but he couldn't shake the notion that he was onto something.

"Talk to my dad before you make any decisions."

She shook her head. "I've already made up my mind."

Just like she had about them. No talking it over. No second chances. Just boom and she'd made a judgment call. And she'd told him in an exam room no less.

"You're going to break her heart."

"It's better than her breaking her neck."

True to Carson's prediction, Bella had been utterly devastated by Ava's decision. Ava had hated dashing her daughter's hopes, but how did she explain that she just didn't trust horses enough to believe they'd take care of her in the middle of a herd of cows? It was scary enough having her ride in an arena during practice. She couldn't imagine her daughter moving a cow out of a herd and somehow making it stay at one end of the arena.

The only thing that had cheered Bella up was when Reese had asked if she could stay behind and help them saddle and bridle horses the rest of the afternoon. Ava suspected he'd offered because he felt bad about getting her daughter's hopes up, but Bella'd been fine with it.

And so that was how Ava found herself alone in her room and, perversely enough, feeling sorry for herself. It wasn't easy being a mom. Sometimes you had to make tough choices and sometimes those choices weren't popular with your kid, but Bella needed to understand that choice came from love. Ava'd never forgive herself if something happened.

"Darn it," she muttered, getting up from the chair where she'd been checking email on her tablet. She turned to the sliding glass door that led to a private terrace. The rooms were elevated slightly, affording guests a nice view. It was framed by redwood rails, which she walked toward and rested her hands on. They still held the heat of the day.

She sighed.

She'd hurt Carson. She could see it in his eyes. But how to explain that taking things slow was necessary for her peace of mind? She would not rush into something again. Not when so much was at stake. In time, when she was a little more comfortable, maybe they could go out on a date.

Maybe.

She focused on the view, tired of thinking about everything so much. Beyond the terrace stretched an emerald-green lawn, and beyond that, a huge pool made to look like an island oasis. Off in the distance she had a view of buttes and desert cacti, and a stunning sunset that painted everything with strokes of reds and yellows and oranges. It smelled good, too. Like honeysuckle or something, and she wondered if one of the cacti that dotted the property was in bloom. She just wished she had some wine. She supposed she could order some. She could afford life's little luxuries now. The days of scrimping and saving while trying to graduate from college were over. Come to think of it, this was the first time she and Bella had been on vacation in… Wow, she couldn't think back to how long.

Someone knocked on her door.

She jumped, wondering if it was Bella. Ava had texted her the room number when she'd checked in. Reese and Carson would bring her back once they were done working the horses at the show grounds, but she didn't expect them for at least another hour. They'd mentioned something about grabbing a bite to eat.

"Ava?" a voice called from the other side.

Carson.

Her heart just about thrust itself from her chest. Goodness gracious, she didn't want to see him, especially since she knew that he was here to see her about Bella. She just knew her daughter had begged him to help change Ava's mind. It would be so like her.

Should she pretend to be out? But no. She'd never been a wimp, wouldn't start now.

Still, her pulse throbbed at her neck as she opened the door. "Hey."

He hadn't changed from the stable, the smell of horses and sweat clinging to him. It shouldn't be a pleasant smell and yet, for some strange reason, it was.

"Can we talk?"

About them? "Is it about Bella? I told you what my decision was about that."

She saw him take a deep breath. "No, not just Bella."

She almost told him no, but in the end she figured she owed him some kind of explanation for giving him the brush-off this week.

She swung the door wide. He walked in, surveying her room. "Nice." His gaze lingered on the bungalow-style furniture, catching for a moment on the bed.

It was like someone held a torch up to her cheeks. Standing there, his handsome face in profile, it reminded her of their night together.

It's not going to happen again.

"I was just out on the terrace." She headed to the sliding glass door at the end of the room. Air. She needed air. And to escape the presence of that bed. "Maybe we should talk out there."

He followed and for that she was grateful.

"Nice view," he said, taking a seat on a rattan chair.

"Yeah, but I think your view is better."

He tipped his head in confusion.

"At your dad's house. You must have a great view from your room."

His eyes held her own and she wished she knew what he was thinking. He wasn't happy with her. That much she could glean.

"I don't live in that house, remember? I live with my brothers and cousin, but one day I *will* have this." He sat back, the brim of his hat nearly touching the chair. "I plan to build a home on my family's property. And while we're on the subject, I'm not exactly broke, you know. My dad's not the type to hand things to his kids, so we get a salary for working at the ranch. Then there's my rodeo earnings. I don't earn as much now as I will in the future, but rodeos pay pretty well as long as you do enough of them. I've been able to put away all my earnings and it's enough to pay for the land I plan to purchase

from my dad. Then I'll build a house, my dream house."
He peered at her from beneath the brim of his hat. "And
I'll pay cash for that, too."

She had to look away from him because, damn it, he
made her feel bad. As if she was superficial.

Aren't you?

She had to do some deep analysis then because she'd
never cared about a person's social status. Carson's hadn't
bothered her.

Or had it.

She gulped.

Maybe she did mind his laid-back, cowboy attitude.
Maybe the fact that he worked for his dad bothered her
a little, too. And that, by all accounts, he hadn't taken
his rodeo career seriously.

"I do have a steady income, Ava. And it'll be a good
one, too, when I get back to the rodeo circuit. But I'm
not here to boast about my prospects. Well, not entirely.
I'm mainly here because Bella asked me to come talk to
you about riding Snazzy tomorrow."

Of course he was. But his words still stung, more so
because she admitted it was true. Deep down inside she
had thought him inferior. Wow. Crazy to admit she'd
been a snob.

"It wasn't just the job," she said softly. "It was everything."

She couldn't deal with another risk-taking, fun-loving,
not-a-care-in-the-world man in her life. Once had nearly
killed her.

"What does any of it matter?" He stared straight
ahead. "I'm not Paul."

"I know that."

"Do you?"

He held her gaze. She saw emotions flit through them. Sadness. Disappointment. Maybe even anger.

"You're not Paul," she admitted. "But you're like him in so many ways." She realized she was close to tears all of a sudden. "You ride horses. He liked to base jump. You like to compete in a sport that's dangerous. He loved to climb mountains. You're probably never home. He was always dashing off to conquer some kind of challenge. I can't deal with that."

"I'm not Paul," he said again.

"I know, but I'm still terrified of what dating someone like you might do to me."

"Is that why you won't let Bella ride?"

Her gaze jerked to his. "What do you mean?"

"Are you worried she'll become addicted to the adrenaline, like her father? That you'll somehow lose her to the sport?"

"No." That wasn't the case at all.

She clutched the rattan chair, her vision whitening she stared straight ahead for so long.

Was it?

She sensed rather than saw him move. He'd scooted his chair closer.

"Let her ride, Ava. She's good. She's going to be great, if only you'll let her fly."

Like she'd let Paul fly. Oh, dear goodness, he *was* right. She *was* holding Bella back. The Gillians would never put her in harm's way. She knew that deep inside. Her heart pounded so hard she wondered if he could hear it. "Okay."

He straightened. "You won't regret it."

Was he talking about Bella riding? Or them? She looked away. Her hands actually shook.

What a hypocrite.

How many times had she told her patients not to be afraid, that they were in good hands, *her* hands? Now she couldn't even trust herself.

"Thanks for listening." He stood. "You've got a pretty special kid. I'm glad you're not afraid to let her spread her wings."

He turned away. She stood, too. "Carson."

He kept walking.

"I'm so sorry."

Were those tears forming in her eyes? Oh, hell. "I'm so afraid. Of you. Of us. Of where this might lead."

He stopped at last, slowly turned and stared at her for the space of five heartbeats—she counted every one of them pumping in her chest.

"And you think I'm not?"

"No. I mean yes. Oh, I don't know." She wiped at her eyes. "I didn't mean to hurt you, but I can see that I did."

"You did."

This man. He brought out the best in her, and the very worst. Still, she couldn't seem to stop herself from taking a step toward him no matter how hard her heart thumped and how frightened she was of the future.

"Don't go."

His eyes flicked. "Why should I stay?"

"Because if you go, we'll always wonder what might have happened." She took another step.

"You hurt me," he admitted.

Yes. She had. It still lingered in his eyes.

"I won't ever do that again."

She closed the distance between them. He wouldn't make it easy on her, though, didn't move, not even when she raised herself on tiptoe so she could kiss him. It had the same effect on her as before. Her body reacted as if it'd been licked by flames.

Damn him.

He didn't react, just stood there. She pulled back, looked into his eyes.

"Please," she said softly.

It was as if the lever holding back his control suddenly broke. He tugged her to him, kissed her, hard, nearly punishingly, and she let him. Dear Lord, she wanted him to do that, and she realized this time would be different than before. There was no splint on his arm. She wouldn't be in charge of their union. She saw his need to be the one in control in his eyes, to do things to her that he'd wanted to do that first night but couldn't because of his injury.

"Carson..."

She didn't know what she wanted to say, just felt the need to ground herself in the present. He pushed her back up against the bed and she let him, his hands moving to the snap of his jeans, unzipping himself.

Ava lay on the bed. He stood above her, undressing. She tipped her head back and closed her eyes. He all but ripped her clothes off next and she gasped at how good it felt to have him take charge, to be controlled, to let him do to her anything he wanted. Had it ever been like this with Paul? She didn't think it had, could never recall wanting to cry out in pleasure just from a mere touch of fingers, especially when they slid downward, finding her center and causing her to moan.

Her hips lifted and she knew he wanted to watch her, that he needed to be the one in control, and she wanted that, too, moaning as his fingers worked their sweet magic and she began to climb higher and higher.

Lord oh Lord.

How did he do it? How did he get every muscle in her body to quiver? Her legs to shake. Her heart to pound.

He removed his fingers and something new touched her. His mouth…

"Carson" she moaned because she didn't want to do this alone, but he wouldn't let her move. He was her lover. A maestro. A master magician. She gave up trying to scoot away, was too far gone to want to do anything more than let him bring her closer and closer…

"Carson," she cried when her whole body shook one final time. She arched her back, surrendered to his touch in a way she'd never done before, time and space and the very room they were in fading away. There were just the ripples of pleasure that fanned from her center to every nerve ending in her body and Ava knew she'd never be the same again.

Chapter 17

What the hell was wrong with him?

Carson sat up quickly, pulling on his clothes. "I should probably skedaddle before my dad gets back with Bella." His heart had begun to pound. "Big day ahead of her tomorrow."

She stopped him before he could stand. "Carson, are you okay?"

His brow began to sweat. "I'm fine." He pulled on his shirt next, his elbow aching a bit. She watched him the whole time.

"Don't you want to… I mean, are you sure you want to leave?"

He paused for a moment because the look on her face made his heart beat in a funny way. He found himself leaning down, kissing her without even thinking about it.

"No. I don't need anything. That was for you," he said softly. "Only you."

Her eyes widened. "Oh."

He finished dressing, wanted to kiss her again before he left. Truth be told he didn't trust himself, the pressure in his chest beginning to build.

"Thank you," she said.

She must have realized how that sounded because her expression turned sheepish. "Not for that." He watched as her teeth raked her lips. "Although that was nice." She looked away for a moment. "Really nice." She took a deep breath. "Thank you for fighting for Bella. For not getting mad at me when I made a stupid decision. For caring enough to not give up."

His heart lurched. That was the only way to describe it. It just thudded in his chest and he knew as he stared down into her pretty green eyes and smoothed back her mussed dark hair that she was it for him. *It.*

"I'll see you tomorrow."

She drew back. He saw her eyes flicker and for one horrible moment he thought she might question him further. That maybe somehow she'd guessed the panic in his heart.

"Tomorrow," she echoed.

He got out of there so quickly he wouldn't be surprised if his shirt was inside out. He drove like a bat out of hell back to the show grounds only to learn his dad had already left with Bella to take her back to the hotel.

He'd escaped just in the nick of time.

Escaped?

He headed for their trailer. Yes, escaped. He shouldn't have gone to bed with her. It'd triggered something inside him, something that scared the you-know-what out of him.

"You look like a man who needs a drink," Reese said the moment he came into their trailer, taking his hat off and hanging it on the corner of a chair.

He took a deep breath, forced himself to act normal. "Bella get home okay?"

"Oh, yeah." His dad sat on the seat opposite him. One of the spoils of war, their horse trailer with RV quarters in the front of it. The sides popped out, making it as roomy as a lot of homes.

"You talk to the mom?"

More than talk. Carson got up quickly, heading to the refrigerator and pulling out a beer before turning back. "You want one?" he offered before forgetting his dad shouldn't. He was still on a restricted diet from his heart surgery.

"Nah."

He popped the lid, the smell of hops filling the air. Carson took a big swig.

"You like her, don't you?"

He thought about denying it. "Yup."

"Oh, to hell with it, let me have a beer," Reese said. "One's not going to kill me."

Carson retrieved the treat. His dad did the same thing he'd done, taking a big swig. Only he released a huge sigh afterward. "Forgot how much I missed the taste."

Carson sat in his vacated chair. "I think I might be falling in love with her, Dad."

Reese inhaled deeply, rested his free palm atop his belly, which had gotten a little bigger in recent years. "Carson, I'm going to be brutally honest here. Women like Dr. Moore aren't very conducive to a rodeo lifestyle. You know that. You also told me the other day you wanted to make a run for the NFR, and I support that decision. Hell, it's about time. But how do you plan to do that and date a woman at the same time?"

The panic returned. He admitted that was the question that had chased him out of her hotel room. "I would hope we could work it out."

"Are you sure about that, son? What about the weekends you're away? About the weekends when she's away? Hell, the weekdays. Do you know how many hours a doctor works?"

"I know, but she's been doing it alone for a while now."

"And you think that will stop her from resenting your time away?"

His father's words were like a sucker punch. That

was exactly what he feared. How many marriages had he seen break up because of the rodeo lifestyle? One spouse wanted a home and kids. The other wanted to chase gold-buckle dreams.

"You know how tough it was on me and your mother."

And that was the reason for the panic. Because as soon as he'd realized how serious things could get with Ava, he'd been hit by the realization that he might just be heading down the same road as his dad.

"I always wondered if your marriage wasn't part of the reason why she got so sick," Carson admitted with brutal honesty.

"I've wondered the same thing, son."

They'd found a mass in her abdomen. Ironically it hadn't been cancer, but it had caused health problems and she'd died when they'd gone in to remove it. No such thing as routine surgery. He'd learned that the hard way.

"I'd like to give you my blessings, son. Lord knows, the woman is a catch. But I'd be lax in my duties as a parent if I didn't tell you to be cautious. This lifestyle isn't for everyone. If you're not at a rodeo, you're at a horse show. You should at least talk to her about your concerns."

His dad was right. What if Ava got tired of his life on the road? She could have anyone…anyone. What the hell did she see in him? Sure, the sex was good…right now. But all things faded with time. What then?

He hated that he doubted himself. Hated that he'd run out on her the way he had. It made him feel like even more of a failure. Maybe tomorrow he'd have the courage to talk to her.

Maybe.

"I think I'm going to puke."

Ava glanced over at Bella quickly, careful to keep the

SUV on the road. She'd been up at the crack of dawn, long before they'd had to leave, polishing her boots, plucking every speck of lint off her jeans, smoothing the soft cotton of her button-down shirt Reese had bought her yesterday, cleaning her hat. She'd never seen her daughter so focused on something in her life.

"Relax. You're going to be great." Ava took a deep breath, trying to quell her inner fear.

She'll be fine. Carson's words echoed in her ears.

"And even if you have a tough time, it's your first show. You have plenty of time to get better."

Just please don't fall off. Please, please, please.

Out of the corner of her eye she saw Bella glance over at her. "Do I?"

Ava met her gaze for a second. "What do you mean?"

"Do you like Carson, Mommy?"

"Of course I do."

"No." Bella frowned. "I mean *like.* As in, do you think you might want to date him?"

She almost laughed. If Bella only knew.

But the question was a serious one and she needed to think on how to answer. She didn't want to get Bella's hopes up, but she didn't want to lie to her, either. Sooner or later she would have to admit to her relationship with Carson.

"I think there's a definite possibility that I could date him."

"Really?" Bella squealed, spinning to face her. "Oh my gosh, Mom, that would be so cool. Maybe I could ride more. You could leave me at Gillian Ranch. I'm sure they wouldn't mind if I started doing extra stuff to help out. That would give you some alone time—"

"Whoa." Ava laughed. "Slow down there, partner. Things will happen when they happen."

"But do you think we could go over there more?"

So Ava could spend time with Carson. Where? she wondered. In the bunkhouse he shared with his brothers and cousin? That would be romantic.

She shoved the thought away. "We'll talk to Carson about it later."

That seemed to satisfy her daughter. Ava bit back a smile, one that faded as they pulled in to the equestrian facility a short time later. Her nerves had returned in full force.

"One day, I want a place just like this."

Ava smiled. "That's a nice dream."

Bella pinned her with a stare. "You watch. I'll have a place just like this one day."

She stared at the determination in her daughter's eyes and suddenly didn't doubt it. "You have good taste. This place is beautiful."

"It is," Bella said. "Mr. Gillian told me the owners are big-time cutting people. They travel all over the country. So does Flynn, Carson's brother. He couldn't come to this show, which is why Carson is here. That's pretty much all Carson's dad does these days, cutting horse competitions. That's what Carson told me yesterday."

They entered the facility and though it'd dawned a chilly desert morning, inside almost felt warm.

"I forgot to tell you, Mommy, that yesterday, when I was riding in the arena, people were asking who I was. It was so cool. I felt like a celebrity. Everyone knew who Snazzy was. I guess she's won a ton of stuff and I get to ride her."

Because of Carson. Because of the whole Gillian family, actually. Ava couldn't begin to put into words how much that meant to her. Sure, she was terrified of her daughter competing, but it was outweighed by the joy on Bella's face. She'd never seen her so animated. And the bad dreams she'd been having? Gone. She supposed she had Carson to thank for that.

"Good morning," Reese Gillian said when he realized they'd arrived. He looked at Bella. "You excited?"

"I think I'm going to puke," she said again.

"That's only normal."

Carson came out of the tack room then, a bridle over his arm, and their gazes connected with the force of a lightning rod. She felt herself blush. He'd left so suddenly yesterday, but she'd been grateful when, not ten minutes after he was gone, Bella had knocked on their hotel room door.

"Is there anything she should be doing?"

Carson shook his head. "I've already got Snazzy all tacked up. All you need to do is get on and practice a little. Class starts in a half hour."

"Mom," Bella said. "I forgot my hat in the car."

"I'll go get it."

It was one thing after another after that. Bella needed a brush next. She needed Ava to pick up her competition number from the show office. Could she help do her hair? Was her shirt buttoned right?

Ava was okay with playing fetch-and-carry because, truth be told, she was probably more nervous than her daughter. Horses still scared her—something about their size still freaked her out—so she kept her distance. She preferred to hang back and watch as Carson reviewed with Bella what she'd be doing in the arena. Bella had told her they'd already gone over it at least a dozen times. From what Ava understood, all Bella had to do was pick a cow out of a herd and stop it from returning to its friends. Simple.

"You want to go watch from the grandstands?" Carson's dad asked her. "I think Carson's going to stay with Bella to help steady her nerves."

"Sure," Ava said. Then to Bella she asked, "Are you okay if I leave?"

"Mom, I'll be fine. Me and Carson have got this."

Reese smiled at Ava. "I'll meet you up there, then. Going to grab us a couple waters real quick. You go on ahead and find a seat before it gets too crowded."

Easier said than done. The place was a maze with all the stalls. She headed toward the center, figuring that was the most likely place for an arena. She turned out to be wrong. The whole left side of the building was where horses and riders competed, stalls taking up the right side.

"All right, everyone," said a man over a loudspeaker. "Fifteen-minute call to the first class. Order of go is posted. Make sure you're at the back gate and ready. First rider out, remember to stay in the arena and help settle the herd after your go."

Fifteen minutes. By the time she found a seat in the grandstands along the short side of the building, she understood why Reese had asked her to find somewhere to sit. The place was packed. In the arena a herd of young cows stood huddled together, some of them calling out, others moving around. Two mounted cowboys kept them at the end opposite where she sat. A scoreboard hung above them. Bella would go fifth in the class. Carson said that was good. For some reason you didn't want to go first, although no one had told her why.

"How do you think Hannah's going to do?" she heard a woman ask another woman sitting behind her. "That new horse of hers working out?"

"He's great," the woman said, "but there's no way in hell it'll beat that Gillian horse. Oh, well. Not much you can do about it."

"You never know," said the friend. "I hear the little girl who's riding it is new to cutting. She could easily make a mistake or two."

"I heard the same thing. And that Carson Gillian is screwing the mom, which is how the little girl scored such a nice ride."

Ava couldn't help herself. She turned, but the two women were in their own little world. One was a bleached blonde who had more sparkles on her shirt than a disco ball. The other was a brunette who wasn't dressed as flashy as her friend but wore enough silver jewelry to drown herself if she happened upon a flood.

"I wouldn't mind doing Carson if it meant a better ride for my kid."

"No kidding, right?" said the blonde. "But you know how it is with Carson. It never lasts very long."

"I don't know. This time he might hang around. Heard the mom's a doctor. Makes a lot of money. Carson likes them wealthy. Remember Katarina? Means he doesn't have to work as hard. Or so I've heard."

That did it. Ava stood. She wanted—oh, how she wanted—to turn around and give the women a piece of her mind. Instead she scanned the bleachers for a different place to sit, somewhere far away from the two sniping women, but she made eye contact with the blonde as she turned away. She might have held the woman's gaze a bit longer than what was polite, too, but she just didn't care.

Screwing Carson so Bella had a good horse to ride. Her heart was beating so fast from a surge of anger-driven adrenaline that her hands shook. And Carson screwing her for her money. He wasn't doing that.

Was he?

No, she quickly told herself, finding a place to sit all the way on the other side of the grandstand. That wasn't the case at all. Carson wasn't that way. Plus, he'd told her himself that he had plenty of his own money. Those women were just repeating gossip and, like most rumors, it wasn't true.

She hoped.

Chapter 18

He'd spotted her sitting in the bleachers with his dad. Carson absently patted Snazzy's neck as Bella awaited her turn. Ava looked pale sitting up there and he knew it had to be hard for her to watch Bella when she was so afraid of horses.

"That black steer looks pretty good," Bella said.

Carson looked up at her and for a moment he forgot about his troubles and what he was going to do about Ava. Bella wore a black cowboy hat and a turquoise button-down, a paisley scarf around her neck with purples and greens and blues. It all combined to make her look like a seasoned pro. Her observation about the black steer was spot-on, too. He'd noticed the same steer during the first run.

"That one and the brindle look pretty good, I'm thinking."

She nodded, eyes intently studying the herd of steers. Amazing that she'd just started to ride a few weeks ago. And that she so quickly understood the intricacies of a cutting horse competition.

"I see my mom," Bella said, waving.

Ava waved back and, for some reason, he suddenly felt tense, and he had no idea why. He'd been to dozen of these things. Nobody expected Bella to win. That'd be a huge surprise. But he wanted Bella to win, he admitted, wanted to impress the heck out of Ava with his training skills.

"Okay," he said, looking up at Bella. "Let's trot her around a moment. Your turn is coming up."

Bella nodded, turning Snazzy around and then kicking her into a trot. He watched her ride, marveling at how well she sat in the saddle already. He'd thought about putting her in a beginner class, but Snazzy was no beginner cutting horse and so he didn't think that'd be fair to the other riders. So Bella was riding in the youth cutting against seasoned competitors and he hoped like hell she didn't fall off. Ava would probably have a heart attack.

"Is she ready?" asked the ring steward.

"As she'll ever be," Carson quipped, waving Bella over.

"Good luck," he said, winking at her.

She seemed petrified. For a moment he wondered if she'd chicken out. He should have known better. The kid was a chip off the old block, squaring her shoulders and lifting her chin. Snazzy's head came up when the gate opened. The old cow horse knew how the game was played. She'd take good care of his girl.

His.

He smiled. She did feel sort of like his kid. He'd gotten close to her in the preceding weeks. He just hoped she remembered everything he'd taught her.

He shouldn't have worried. She took her sweet time assessing the cattle, finding the black steer they'd been talking about earlier, which had retreated deep into the herd—a stroke of luck on their part. She had to cut at least one steer that wasn't along the edges or in front. Snazzy seemed to read her young rider's mind, heading straight for the animal in question, and Bella sat so quietly in the saddle it seemed as if she used mind control.

"Atta girl," he said softly. "Ease it away."

He glanced at the clock. Over a minute still left to work. Plenty of time to put on a show. And show off she did, because once Bella had the steer off on its own, it tried like the dickens to return to its friends. But Snazzy and Bella kept it back, the horse ducking left then right and then left again, and Bella hanging on like she'd been born into the sport.

"Atta girl," he said more loudly, whistling his approval.

He saw Bella glance at the clock, knew she'd remembered she had to cut at least one more steer from the herd, maybe even two, time permitting. She went after the brindle next and, if anything, the damn thing was better than the first, the crowd erupting into applause when Snazzy did a quick duck left and then right, like a prize fighter avoiding a blow. The steer ran. Snazzy did, too, and Carson's heart was in his throat when Bella slid back in the saddle.

Too fast.

If Snazzy hit the brakes, Bella might fall off. His hands gripped the railing, but the darn kid hung on. She regained her seat and the crowd roared its approval when Snazzy swung back in the other direction at a million miles per hour. Well, not that fast, but it seemed like it to Carson, who felt like he might have a heart attack. Was this how his dad felt when one of his kids competed? If so, he had a whole new respect for the old man.

With thirty seconds left on the clock, Bella pulled Snazzy up. He thought she might call it, but no, the kid picked a third steer, a little brown-and-white that quickly took off. Snazzy was right on her tail. Carson had no idea how she managed to hold the thing back, but Bella did, and when the buzzer sounded Carson found himself jumping up on the fence, clapping so hard his palms stung, and yelling, "Good job, Bella!" as loud as he could.

She must have heard him, because Bella turned toward him, her smile so wide it nearly matched the brim of her hat. She looked as excited as a kid who'd discovered a pony on Christmas morning. And as he stared into Bella's brilliant eyes, an ache began to build in his chest. It was the strangest sensation, and it only grew the closer Bella got to him.

"I did it!" she squealed.

"Yes, you did."

The ache turned into a softness and the softness into an emotion so pure, he instantly knew what it was. Love.

It was the same thing he'd felt last night as he'd stared into Ava's eyes.

Ava made her way down to Bella as quickly as she could, but not before making eye contact with the two women in the grandstand. They stared at her curiously as she passed by and she knew it wasn't nice of her, but she hoped they watched her walk up to Carson and that they'd realize she'd been sitting in front of them.

"I am so proud of you," Carson was saying as she walked up.

"Did you see my score? Seventy five. I was just hoping to break into the sixties."

Ava hung back for a moment. Carson stared into Bella's eyes and the pride on his face—and also the joy—made her watch him for a second, transfixed. If ever she wondered if a man could love Bella as much as she did, the answer was right there in Carson's face.

"Mom!"

She hadn't even noticed Bella turning toward her. She was off Snazzy and tossing Carson the reins before she could blink, nearly knocking her hat off her head when she threw herself into Ava's arms.

"Wasn't that great!"

"It was amazing," Ava said, hugging her and closing her eyes and wondering why she felt so completely out of sorts. "You were perfect."

"Well, not perfect. I could have held on to that second steer a little longer. It started to get away from me and I chickened out so I took a third. Carson said I should have stuck with the two."

And listen to her sounding so professional. Even more surprising, Ava understood what she was saying.

"You did great."

"Do you think I'll win?" Bella asked, turning back to Carson.

"I think it's too early to tell. There's quite a few more kids to go."

"It doesn't matter," Bella said, heading back to Snazzy. "You're such a good horse." She leaned in and hugged the horse's head and Ava marveled at how Bella could be so completely horse crazy when she hadn't been raised around them.

Carson's gaze met her own.

She forgot all about Bella and horses and the people around them. Why did it always feel this way when she looked at him? Like she was about to zip-line across a canyon.

"I'm proud of her," he said.

Her heart flipped over for a whole other reason. "Me, too."

Bella had one of the highest scores of the class, right up until the end when a girl who had to be at least five years older than Bella came in and blew the crowd away. Ava and Reese watched from the grandstand while Bella and Carson put Snazzy away.

"Oh, well," Reese said as they made their way to the

barn. "She still got second. That's pretty remarkable for her first show in that deep a competition."

"She's ecstatic." Someone waved at Reese. It seemed as if everyone knew who Reese was. They hadn't been in the grandstand thirty seconds before someone had sat next to him and started talking. It hadn't stopped since.

"Thank you so much for this, Reese." Ava motioned around them. "I feel so blessed to have met you and the family. Bella is in heaven."

"She's a good kid," Reese said. "You should start thinking about getting her a horse."

She nodded. "I've had the same thought."

"You know, Snazzy's for sale."

Ava nodded. "I'm almost afraid to ask the price."

"I'll make you a deal."

She had a feeling even a "deal" would be way out of her price range. "Let me know how much of a deal and we'll talk."

"Fair enough." Reese waved to someone else. "You two going to the wine and cheese thing tonight?"

She had no idea. She'd overheard someone talking about it, but she and Bella hadn't discussed the matter.

"I don't know. I'll have to ask Bella."

"I might have her get up on some of our other horses tonight, after the show's over. You mind if she's a little late?"

"She'd love that."

"Good for her, too. Helps to ride more than one horse. Build her legs." Someone waved Reese over and he smiled. "Got to go. If you want, leave Bella here. She'll learn a lot by hanging out and watching other runs today."

He left her then and Ava wondered if the old rancher was trying to give her some alone time with his son, and if so, why? Carson had been pretty quiet this morning—well, other than when Bella had come out of the ring—but he hadn't seemed anxious to get her alone again. Not that she wanted that, not with Bella around. They would need to think about how to tell her daughter about the two of them.

"Mom, look at this!" Bella ran to her, a ribbon with red streamers in her hand. "Second place."

She looked as excited as if she'd gotten first. Her hair was creased where her hat had sat and one of her cheeks had a streak of dirt on it, but Ava had never seen her child so happy. It warmed her heart, made her think she was just overthinking things where Carson was concerned.

"That's great, honey."

"Carson said he's going to take me out to dinner to celebrate, but not tonight because tonight you have the wine and cheese thing."

"I don't have to go to that," Ava said.

"No, Mom. Go. I want you to go. And Kylie said I could hang with her tonight."

"Kylie? Who's Kylie?"

"She was in the class before mine. The novice class. We met while I was waiting at the back gate. She's really nice. They're staying at the same hotel."

"I don't know—"

"Please, Mom?"

If she were honest with herself, Ava sort of wanted to go by herself. When was the last time she'd dressed up for an occasion? Let her hair down. Do an adult-type thing? It'd been ages.

"And Carson's dad said I could stay here this afternoon if I wanted to," she added. "Can I do that, too?"

"I don't see why not."

It would give Ava time to find a mall because suddenly she didn't think anything she'd brought was good enough to wear. Might as well go all out.

"Cool. I'll go tell Kylie I can hang with her tonight."

"Wait." She hadn't said that part was okay, but her kid was off and running. She watched her dash over to a young girl who Ava could tell was her age.

She'd found a friend.

Something had happened to her child. She exuded confidence all of a sudden. It came from the way she held herself now. Tall. Proud.

Thoroughly happy.

Horses had given Bella something Ava never would have thought possible and she had Carson and his family to thank for it. They'd welcomed them with open arms, changed Bella's life and for that she would forever be grateful.

So she checked in with Kylie's mom later on, and she could tell instantly that she liked her. It helped when she heard that the Gillians were old family friends. She was on her own.

She didn't see Carson when she left. That was okay. She'd see him later.

And if that afternoon she spent a little too much money on a cream-colored frilly lace shirt made to look like roses around the low-cut neckline, so what? The lady at the Western store said it was perfect for the occasion, especially when paired with a dark brown mermaid skirt that had similar embellishments along a slit that ended midthigh. She'd even bought her first pair of fancy boots.

She heard from Carson just before she left, and it was silly how her heart leaped and that a smile came to her face. He said he'd meet her at the venue, the home of the owners of the ranch. And so she dressed in her new outfit and pulled her hair back, looping it around and then securing it in such a way that the straight ends fanned out behind her.

Her stomach fluttered as she pulled up to a stunning brick mansion with its private entrance, one far enough away from the equestrian center that all you could glimpse was the red roof in the distance, a massive pasture in between. It was still sunny outside and the view of the oaks and horses grazing in the distance was beautiful. A valet came forward to park her vehicle, and Ava felt out of place all of sudden as she headed for the double-wide front door made entirely of glass and framed by elegant wrought-iron scrolls. She should have sent Carson a text message and asked him to meet her out front, but she was a grown woman. She could enter a room all on her own.

"Welcome," said an older woman with a wide smile and a simple white button-down shirt and jeans that made Ava wonder if she might be overdressed.

"Thank you." She smiled.

"You're with Gillian Ranch, aren't you?" said the woman. "Dr. Ava Moore?"

Ava tried to hide her surprise. "I am. In a way. My daughter rides there."

The woman's grin was friendly and filled with approval. "Well, your daughter is a very lucky little girl. You should buy that horse she rode if you can. Reese Gillian is very picky about who gets to purchase his animals."

Was he?

The woman moved on to the next guest and Ava entered a massive foyer where people were dressed in an odd mixture of riding clothes and fancy Western attire. Good. At least she wasn't overdressed.

The room smelled faintly of roses and horses, and it felt as if every pair of eyes was on her. The new kid on the block. She turned, thinking she'd get a drink, and there was Carson, standing next to one of the women from the grandstand, although he wasn't looking at her. He had eyes only for Ava. She saw him bend without looking away, watched as he clearly said, "Excuse me," and then walked in Ava's direction. And Ava was vain enough to love the way the woman followed the direction of his gaze, her eyes narrowing when she saw her standing there.

"Wow," he said when he got close enough, and yet there was something in his gaze, something that made her study him closely.

"Wow to you," she said right back. He wore a black cowboy hat with a starched white shirt and jeans, but he'd shaved and his blue eyes gleamed as they eyed her up and down.

"You went shopping."

Was he worried about people thinking she was his girlfriend? Was the way he stood back his way of giving her more space?

"I wasn't sure what to wear."

Something flickered in his eyes. "You look perfect."

And she just about melted. It'd been a long, long time since she'd been made to feel appreciated and desired. The look in Carson's eyes made her toes curl.

"Let me introduce you around." He placed a hand at her back and she instantly felt better.

They made the rounds, Ava knowing she'd never remember a single name. Well, all but one. Melissa Watson was one of the ladies from the grandstand, the blonde one, and her first impression of her didn't improve.

"So you're the one whose kid beat mine," she said with a smile as fake as the diamonds around her neck. Okay. So maybe they weren't fake, but they were gaudy.

"I guess so," Ava said with a smile as fake as her own.

"Carson, a little birdie tells me you'll be making a

bid for the NFR again now that your elbow's all healed," said the blonde.

"I am," Carson said. "Figured it's time I get off my butt and live up to the family name. Even entered a rodeo at the end of the month."

A rodeo? What?

"But you just started therapy," said the doctor in her.

"I'm not sure I need that," he hedged. "It's feeling pretty good."

She knew that wasn't true, she'd seen him rubbing his arm earlier, and she wanted to call him out on it, but she couldn't, not now. So she bit her tongue, but it irked her. If he skipped therapy, there was no telling what kind of damage he might do to his arm. It might ruin his chance of ever roping again. Or swinging a hammer. Or doing any number of things to support himself. Why would he risk that?

"So that means you'll be heading back out on the rodeo trail soon," Melissa said. "How exciting." She turned to Ava. "Does that mean you'll be going with him on the road?"

Ava tried to maintain her smile. "Actually, no. I have to work."

The woman nodded as if she hadn't known that Ava was a doctor, and Ava decided she really didn't like her. Not at all.

"That's too bad." She smiled up at Carson. "I know how lonely you cowboys get on the road."

Was that an invitation to call her when loneliness struck? Or a warning? Ava didn't know, didn't care. At least, that was what she told herself.

"Nice to meet you." Ava hooked an arm through Carson's and walked away.

"You can't skip therapy."

"I can't stand that lady," he whispered in an aside.

"I won't let you."

He stopped.

She stared up at him. "Carson, if you skip therapy, you might do permanent damage to your arm. Isn't that important to you?"

"Not as important as getting a start on qualifying." He glanced around, probably worried someone would overhear them. "Besides, if things don't work out, I'll build furniture or something."

"With one arm?"

He wouldn't look at her.

"Carson. This is serious. It's your whole future."

"No. I can ride horses for a living if I have to. It's not as glamorous as rodeo, but it's a living and I can do other things, too."

And live in discomfort for the rest of his life. He might not know what that was like, but she did. Chronic pain was nothing to mess with. It could lead to other more dangerous problems. Depression. Anger. Addiction. And for what? A chance at a gold buckle.

It made her ill.

And if he was willing to risk so much just in the hope of making it to the NFR, what else was he willing to give up?

That made her even sicker.

Chapter 19

She'd gone all quiet on him. In his experience that boded ill for the male species.

"You okay?" he asked.

He saw her take a deep breath. "I think I need a glass of wine."

He nodded. "I'll go get you one. Meet me out on the patio?"

"Sure."

She was mad about his elbow, and about him skipping therapy, and probably even entering that rodeo. He supposed he didn't blame her, but it made him wonder if he realized how important this was to him.

Night had fallen. It took a moment for his eyes to adjust, but her off-white shirt was easy to spot beneath the covered patio that overlooked a softly lit pool. They were alone for the most part, Ava sitting in a chair that looked more like something you'd find indoors rather than out.

"Here you go," he said, handing her a glass of white wine. "No Zinfandel tonight. Sorry."

"That's okay," she said and then took a sip.

She looked like something out of a television show, the kind that featured well-dressed women and exotic locales. The light from the pool gently brushed her cheeks, one side in shadow, the other not, the green in her eyes nearly the same color as the pool to his right. Her gaze seemed huge when painted by shadows and he wished he could read what she was thinking, because something about her posture told him she was upset. He took a seat near her, a small table separating them.

"When were you going to tell me you wanted to skip therapy?"

Just as he'd thought. "I don't know. I guess I didn't think it was that important."

"It's important to me."

"Is it?"

She didn't immediately answer. Took another sip of her wine.

"I guess I just can't believe you're willing to risk permanent damage to your arm all so you can compete. It boggles my mind, I suppose. What would it hurt to wait a few weeks?"

And there it was, exactly as his dad had predicted, their first disagreement over his rodeo lifestyle. "Ava, it's fine."

"No, it's not. Your bones are still healing. If you fell off now, you could destroy your elbow. I'm telling you, Carson, you shouldn't do it. But don't take my word for it. Go see another doctor if you think I'm overreacting."

"I don't think you're overreacting. I get why you're upset."

"Oh, yeah? Then why do it?"

Because he was an excellent horseman. He hadn't fallen off in years. Well, except for the last time, but before that it'd been years.

"Because I really think I'll be fine."

The answer seemed to disappoint her. "Look, when you get back to town, let's take another X-ray. I'll be able to tell you better how you're healing then. No. Don't say anything. That's the deal. Take it or leave it."

Take it or leave it? "Or what?"

She looked away for a moment. "Or…nothing. I don't know. Just do this for me."

Demands. Ultimatums. Already they were sounding like his mom and dad. "Okay."

He'd planned to tell her how he felt about her tonight; instead he held is tongue. His own irritation left a hole in his stomach.

"Thank you," she said softly.

He took a swallow of his wine, told himself to calm down, and with her staring at him so imploringly, and relief in her eyes working as a balm to his frustration, he found himself bending to kiss her softly. And, as it always did, it turned into much, much more. He set his drink down.

"Let's get out of here," he said a long while later.

"And go where?"

He smiled. "Well, it just so happens the resort had a cancellation so I reserved a room for the two of us. We have our own place for the night." She tensed. "Or for a few hours. Whatever you're comfortable with. I'll take what I can get."

"Okay," she said breathlessly. "Let's go."

I'll take what I can get.

The question was, could she? Not now, but later, when he was back on the road again.

It was a thought that repeated itself the next day as she and Bella drove home from the horse show, Bella so exhausted from showing a horse and hanging out with Kylie she instantly fell asleep in the passenger seat, her pretty red ribbon clasped to her chest. That was good. It gave Ava time to think.

So what if he went against her wishes? He was a grown man. He could make his own mistakes.

Except...

It did bother her. Terribly. She'd taken one step forward, and now it felt like she'd taken a step back. And if he didn't listen to her, that would be another step back. And if he decided to go against her wishes, yet another. She couldn't be with a man who didn't value her professional opinion.

He didn't get back from the horse show until late Sunday night, which meant the next time they'd meet was in her office. Ava didn't give him a choice. She made arrangements from her home, called Radiology, got him set up for an X-ray and made room for him on her calendar. She texted him the schedule, wondered if he'd show up. She was relieved when she checked in with Radiology that morning and learned he was there.

Yet when the time came for them to meet, her stomach felt as tight as the day she'd sat for her medical boards. She absently pulled up the X-ray on her tablet, walking toward her office, her heart beginning to pound.

A dark shadow on the X-ray made her stop. She switched to the next view. It looked no better. Neither did the next one, she thought, walking forward again.

Something of what she felt must have showed on her face when she opened the door.

"What's the matter?" He looked so tense, some of her irritation with him faded.

"Hang on."

"Ava."

She ignored him, sitting behind her desk and quickly opening up his file and searching the images they'd taken the first day she'd seen him. Next, she pulled up the new ones. Viewing them on a bigger screen side by side. It only made the bad ones look worse.

"Damn," she muttered.

He leaned forward. "What the hell's going on?"

She hoped he couldn't see the way her hand shook as she aimed the screen toward him. "This is what's going on." She took a deep breath. "More specifically, the dark spot there, right at the end of the bone." She pointed. "This is where it connects with your tendon." She tried to project a confident smile even though she felt anything but. "And that darker area…" *Keep your voice even. He'll be okay.* "That usually indicates some damage."

"I don't see anything."

"It's there, and I'm not going to sugarcoat things, Carson. This concerns me. A lot." She tried to convert things into layman's terms. "Sometimes after surgery, scar tissue develops. Sometimes it gets so bad that it affects the tendons and ligaments surrounding the surgery site. I think what I'm seeing here is scar tissue forming near your medial collateral ligament, and the concern is it will get so bad that you'll lose the range of motion in your arm."

"So it hurts a little." He flexed his arm for good measure, but he couldn't quite conceal his grimace of pain. "I had my first therapy session last week. It'll get better with more work."

"No, it won't. It'll get worse over time. You'll be in a lot of pain."

"Then you can do another surgery, after rodeo season is over."

She leaned back, her chair swinging sideways the motion was so abrupt. As if her operating on him was no big deal. As if she'd be his personal physician. Patch him up and send him on his way, meanwhile his elbow would get worse and worse, all so he could win a gold buckle that'd tarnish over time.

"If you like, I can have my boss and the director of ortho take a look."

He must have realized he'd said something wrong because he scooped his hat off his head and ran his fingers through his hair. "Geez, Ava, I'm sorry." He crammed his hat back on. "I'm just surprised is all. It doesn't feel all that bad."

"It never does, but that's why I told you to wait until you're cleared by physical therapy before you enter a rodeo." She tried to keep the I-told-you-so out of her voice. Didn't work.

"When can your boss take a look?"

And now he was second-guessing her diagnosis. Great. Her irritation returned full force.

"I'll have him take a look today if you want." She picked up her tablet again. "He can call you."

"Okay, great."

She stood abruptly.

"Hey, wait." He stood, too. "Maybe I could come over tonight. We could talk about this over dinner."

"No, not tonight." It surprised her how quickly she put him off. She was steaming inside. Couldn't he see that? "It's a school night. Bella always has a lot of homework and I need to help her out. Plus, she still doesn't know about us, remember?"

He didn't say anything for what felt like the world's longest five seconds.

"Okay, sure. I'll call you."

"And I'll have Dr. Eastman call *you*."

She left before he could see how utterly disappointed she was in him, and how close she was to crying.

Chapter 20

Dr. Eastman confirmed her suspicions. He wanted Carson to get an MRI to be sure, but they were both concerned. She left a message for Carson, but when they talked, he seemed distracted, and she was so irritated with him she didn't ask to see him again.

"He's getting ready for his rodeo," Bella announced later that week as she sat at the kitchen table doing homework, a week during which Ava hadn't heard anything from Carson. Not one word. She hadn't seen him, either—the man did a disappearing act whenever she dropped Bella off for lessons.

"He sent me a text message saying he couldn't give me a lesson this weekend. He's competing on the coast." She straightened. "Hey. Can we go?"

So that was it then. He wasn't going to listen to her.

She wanted to get up and call Carson right then. She wanted to give him a list of the terrible things that could happen if he didn't rest his elbow. To remind him what could happen if he fell. Or had to take meds for the rest of his life.

"What day is the rodeo?"

"Saturday." Bella looked up from her homework. She cocked her head sideways. "What's wrong?"

Ava shook her head. Just terribly disappointed. And sad. And hurt.

"Nothing."

Bella set her pencil down. "There's something wrong."

Her need to vent outweighed her need to keep things between her and Carson. "He shouldn't compete. His elbow... There's been a complication."

"You mean, you didn't fix it?"

That stung. "I did my part. But there's scar tissue. I have nothing to do with that. Some people get it and some people don't. Carson's body makes it and it's encroaching on the elbow joint. If he's not careful, it could lead to permanent damage, but he refuses to listen to me about it and, damn it, Bella, I'm upset."

Her daughter's eyes widened at her swear word. Bella's brown eyes seemed to search every line on her face before her gaze met Ava's. "Is that why you've been so uptight this week?"

"I haven't been uptight."

"Mom. You yelled at me when Balto and I were playing outside."

She was about to deny it—not the yelling part—but suddenly her shoulders slumped because Bella was right. She'd been a mess all week.

"I'm sorry," she said instead.

She felt fingers land on her hand, wanted to cry when she saw sympathy in Bella's eyes. "Do you love him, Momma?"

She drew back, a denial on the tip of her tongue. Bella didn't know they were a couple...did she?

Brown eyes peered up at her own. She did. Oh, damn. And suddenly Ava wanted to cry because she realized she did love him, a truth she could no longer deny. There had always been complete honesty between them even when that honesty was inconvenient.

"I think I do," she said softly.

She had no idea she'd closed her eyes until she heard

Bella stand. In the next moment her daughter's arms wrapped around her shoulders.

"Don't cry, Mommy," she said softly. "It's okay. Carson will come around."

How many times had they stood like this over the years? The days when Ava had worked full-time and come home from school exhausted to the point that she'd broken down. The times Bella had woken up in the middle of the night, crying, missing her dad even though she'd never really known him. The days when both of them had been frustrated about never seeing each other and never going out or doing anything fun. They'd gotten through it all. And now a man had entered their lives and look how it all was ending up.

"How did you know?" she asked her daughter. She drew back. "I thought I'd kept my relationship with Carson a secret."

Bella smiled a little. "Mom, I'm not a baby anymore. I knew something was going on."

Ava sighed. She'd ended up with a pretty amazing daughter, one who was better than her in some ways. How, she had no idea. She'd been gone so much when Bella was little it was a miracle she'd turned out normal at all.

"Go see him, Momma." Bella pulled back. "Talk to him."

"I don't think he'll listen, honey."

"Make him."

If only it was that simple. Bella might seem grown-up in a lot of ways, but when it came to men, she was still naive. Lord willing, it would stay that way for a while.

"I'll try calling him again."

"Good," Bella said, pronouncing the word with a nod. "I'll go get your phone."

* * *

He called her back, but it didn't do any good. Ava didn't know what hurt more, the fact that Carson ignored her warnings or the disappointment in Bella's eyes—not in Ava, but in a man she idolized.

"I still want to go watch him compete," Bella said. "Maybe you can talk him out of it."

Ava shook her head. "I'm not going to show up someplace uninvited."

"But we are invited. He asked me before he left. When he told me he couldn't give me a lesson this weekend."

"Bella—"

"Please, Mom? I've never been to a rodeo. I want to go. I think you should try and talk to him there. You have to at least try. You're his doctor."

She didn't owe him anything. Over the week her anger had turned to acceptance, and then to sadness and then a simmering bitterness that it had come to this. For the first time since Paul, she'd fallen in love, and he'd ended up disappointing her in a way that Paul had never done. Worse, he'd let Bella down, too.

"Okay, fine." Because she'd never been one to take things lying down. "We'll go."

She regretted her decision at least a dozen times by the time they left for the fairgrounds where Carson would compete. But Bella was the real reason why she made the long drive. She would not let her daughter down like Carson had. Even if she suspected Bella's reason for wanting to watch Carson compete had less to do with worrying about his health and more to do with some kind of romantic notion that the two of them would take one look at each other and all would be well. In that, too, she'd be doomed to disappointment.

When they finally found Carson at the rodeo grounds

on a cold and overcast morning, he greeted her daughter like a long-lost friend. Her, not so much.

"Hey," he said after releasing Bella from a hug. "You came."

The smile he gave Ava was forced at best. Hers was, too. "We came."

"How's your elbow?" Bella asked.

"Feeling okay," he said, straightening his arm and then flexing it again. "Cold doesn't help."

Neither would throwing a rope, Ava almost said. Or falling off. Instead she held her tongue. Her daughter turned, motioned her eyes toward Carson before saying, "I'm going to find a place for us to sit," and then darted off like a bank robber.

Damn that kid.

"Sorry I haven't been able to see you," he said, patting the horse he stood next to. "Dad's been keeping me pretty busy."

She kept her distance. "It's okay."

No, it isn't.

She tipped her chin up. "I said what I had to say over the phone." Several times. "Your call."

"Ava—"

She stood there, heart beating fast, palms sweating. Couldn't he see how she felt? How his not listening to her advice felt like a slap in the face? How she fought not to cry?

"I need to do this."

"Why?" she heard herself ask, stuffing her hands into the pockets of the jacket she'd worn, afraid he might see her trembling. "I told you the risks. So did Dr. Eastman. You might end up with irreparable damage. All the stuff you do—riding, building furniture, roping—you won't be able to do it, at least not like before. You risk permanent and debilitating damage. Chronic pain. Loss of function. No rodeo is worth that."

"It is to me."

"Why?" she asked again.

He lifted is chin. "Because I need to prove myself."

"To who? The world? Nobody cares if you rope today. Me? I do care. I care a lot."

"Ava, I haven't been riding," he said earnestly. "I've been resting my arm. And it's better now. It hasn't been hurting at all."

Typical man. Just ignore the problem. Everything will be all right.

"So you're going to compete today and you haven't even been practicing?"

"Well, yeah. I thought you'd be happy about that."

She squeezed her eyes shut. Stupid, stupid man. Like his not riding was supposed to make her feel better. He shouldn't even be there.

She felt his hands begin to slip around her. She stepped back, opened her eyes. She hoped he saw the anger within them, and the disappointment.

"Good luck today."

And then she turned and walked away.

He'd blown it.

It'd been the perfect opportunity to tell her he loved her. To confess to her that he didn't want to be Dr. Ava Moore's gigolo. He wanted, needed, to be her equal, at least in some small way. *Carson Gillian, rodeo star.*

"You ready for this?"

Carson looked up from checking Rooster's bridle. Next to him, Hotrod, his brother's horse, pricked his ears.

"As I'll ever be," Carson muttered.

"You been practicing?" Shane asked, looking like his

twin in a pink shirt. Breast cancer awareness day at the rodeo. Everyone would be sporting the color.

"Not really."

Shane had no clue Carson had been grounded. Thank goodness he hadn't been around when Ava was talking to him. He had a feeling his brother would take Ava's side and he didn't need any more pressure on him than there already was.

"I thought you were going to get more serious about roping," Shane said, untying his horse so he could slip on Hotrod's bridle. Carson's hands had shaken when he'd done the same thing a few moments ago.

"I am."

"Don't sound like it."

Hard to practice when you weren't riding. He couldn't tell Shane that, though. It would lead to other questions. Questions he didn't want to answer.

"You worry about your own roping."

"Hey, don't get defensive."

Carson just turned away. "I'm going to check in with the rodeo secretary. Hold Rooster for me."

The grounds were nestled in a small valley, the place seeming to crop up out of nowhere, at least in Carson's mind. Trailers and vehicles, mostly trucks, dotted a pasture that'd been converted into rodeo grounds. The San Selmo Rodeo wasn't a PRCA event and Shane and Carson had gotten a lot of sideways looks when they'd pulled in; he felt even more stares when he checked in with the rodeo secretary. They didn't usually compete at this level and he had a feeling the natives were restless…or resentful. But they needed the practice, and it was an open show, as he'd pointed out to his brother. Fair was fair.

He came back with their numbers, handing one to

Shane. They pinned them to their backs and all too quickly, Shane headed to his horse.

"Let's go," he said, swinging up on Hotrod.

"There he is."

Bella pointed to where Carson and Shane were walking, Shane on his horse, Carson leading Rooster toward the arena.

"And he's not riding," Bella said.

Ava's heart leaped into her throat. Not riding. Carson was on the ground. He was speaking to his brother and the conversation looked to be a little heated.

"What's he doing?" Bella asked.

"I don't know."

Shane turned, called another roper over. She saw the man nod at something Shane said, and Carson waved before he turned and headed back to the trailers.

"Wait. I think he's pulling out."

Ava wanted to cry. "You think?"

"Yeah, he's walking to the trailer area again."

Maybe they were jumping to conclusions. Maybe Carson had forgotten something at the trailer.

"If he's not pulling out, he better hurry back." Ava glanced at Shane and then back at Carson. "They're supposed to go fifth and there're only two teams ahead of them now."

"He won't come back. He decided to listen to you, Mom."

She was right. Bella's look was triumphant when Shane entered the roping pen with another partner, the announcer clarifying for spectators that there'd been a change on the heeling end.

Ava covered her face with her hands. He'd decided not to ride. She wanted to cry.

"Stay here," she told Bella.

Her daughter knew what she was going to do. Ava spotted the look of hope in her eyes. She felt it, too, her heart lifting with every step she took.

He wasn't at the trailer. Rooster was, the horse's halter on, his ears pricking forward when he spotted the human walking toward him. She found Carson in the truck, passenger side, staring straight ahead. He didn't look up when she approached.

She knocked on the window.

He glanced at her, nodded. She tried the door, swung it open. "You didn't ride."

Sharp shake of the head. "Nope."

The hope in her heart had begun to fizzle at the look on his face. "And you're mad at me."

He finally looked her in the eye. "Not at you."

That buoyed her spirits a little. "Thank you."

"You're the doctor."

What was that supposed mean? "It was the right thing to do, Carson. The smart thing."

He stared straight ahead again, folded his leg up so he could rest his damaged arm on his knee, his foot against the glove box, pink shirt wrinkling around the elbow.

"You want to know what I thought when we met?" He took a deep breath. "I thought, man, she sure is pretty, but what the hell would she ever see in a guy like me?"

Oh, Carson. Her throat tightened but she kept quiet, sensing he needed to talk.

"Rodeo's been my life. I didn't realize just how big a part until it was gone." He glanced down at his arm. "Or maybe gone."

"It's not over, Carson. Dr. Eastman thinks arthroscopic surgery will work on your elbow. It'd be in and out, and with some therapy, you could be back in the saddle in a month or two."

"Too late for qualifying for the NFR."

"You don't know that."

He turned to face her again, shaking his head. "Do you know what it takes to qualify?"

No, she didn't know. She didn't know anything about rodeo. "I imagine quite lot."

"I wanted it, Ava. I wanted it *bad*." In his eyes was a look she'd never seen before. "I wanted to do it for you and for Bella. I'm in love with you."

She felt her lips begin to tremble and her eyes got warm. *He loved her.*

"But I can't do this." He shook his head. "I can't see this working out between you and me, especially after what just happened. You don't understand. You clearly do not get how important this is to me."

Her voice shook with unshed tears when she said, "But I do."

"We're just too different. You put broken people back together. I break horses for a living. You come from the city. I'm a country boy at heart. You have your whole future ahead of you. I have no idea what the future holds for me."

"We could find out." She had to swallow a lump in her throat. "Together."

"You think?"

Did she? Did she love him enough to take the chance? To put it all on the line? Her breath hitched because she just didn't know.

"Yeah, that's what I thought."

"No. I mean yes. I mean, I don't know." She inhaled, tried to gather control. "Carson, I love you, too."

He slipped out of the truck, swung toward her in shock.

"I know I do because the thought of you riding again, knowing what was at risk, it killed me. I love you. I don't want to lose you."

Why did it sound like she was pleading with him? It wasn't over between them. *Was it?*

But the answer was there in his eyes. She might love him. He might love her, but it wasn't enough. Not for him. Maybe not for her, either.

Fear.

It held them both back.

"I don't know what to do." She realized she'd started to cry.

"Don't you?" he asked gently.

She didn't want to say goodbye. It seemed stupid to do that. They had so much potential. Didn't they?

"I'm going to switch doctors. I hope that's okay with you. I'll do my surgery and therapy with whoever I pick."

"You don't have to do that."

"Yes, I do." His eyes were filled with sadness. "It'd be too hard to see you."

Her breath hitched again. "So that's it? You're saying goodbye?"

She waited for him to deny it, told herself that she wouldn't let him go, but when he moved toward her, she knew it was over. He pulled her into his arms, one last time.

"Oh, Carson," she cried. "Don't. We don't have to do this. Bella…"

"She can take lessons with Flynn. She'll be all right. You will be, too. This is for the best. You know it is, too," he murmured in her ear. "We're too different, you and I. Just too damn different."

She inhaled the scent of him, tried not to break down

right there in the middle of the rodeo grounds. When he pulled back, she stared into his eyes, eyes filled with unshed tears, too.

"Tell Bella I'll see her at the ranch."

He jumped in the truck again, pulled at the door. She stepped back as he closed it. When he didn't look at her again, she had to turn away. She didn't want him to see her eyes fill with tears, refused to let him know how much this hurt her. She headed back to the grandstand. Bella met her halfway.

"What's wrong?"

"He just broke up with me."

Bella's eyes widened. "I'll go talk to him."

"No, Bella, don't." Ava inhaled, her words thick with unshed tears. "Maybe we just need a break."

"Mom."

"No. I'm all right."

But she wasn't. Not even a little bit. But she hid it from Bella…and cried herself to sleep that night.

Chapter 21

"Mom, it's on!"

Ava took a deep breath, her hands resting on the kitchen counter, a tray of fresh fruit scenting the air with sweetness. She glanced out the window. It was dark, the Christmas lights in her front yard twinkling, their first Christmas with a yard to decorate.

"Hurry. You're going to miss him."

She didn't want to hurry. She didn't want to watch Carson at the NFR. It still hurt to even think about the past few months. She had a feeling it would hurt even worse to see him on TV.

She picked up the tray, taking a deep breath, steeling herself against what was to come. Bella had tried to push them back together. He'd even called. She'd talked to him, but there was too much bitterness in her heart to do much more than ask how he was doing. With time she had come to realize it was better that way. In some ways, Carson had hurt her more than Paul ever had.

"Well here's the Cinderella story of the season," said the television announcer. "Shane and Carson Gillian, the sons of Reese Gillian, a famous team roper in his own right."

"That's right, Brewster. Reese was one half of the Dynamic Duo, Reese and Bob Gillian. Together the pair amassed nearly two dozen NFR buckles over the years."

On the television screen, an image of Shane appeared.

He was backing into the box already, swinging his rope, and then the picture changed.

Carson.

"There he is," Bella said excitedly. Balto jumped up, a puzzled look on his face as he stared up at the little girl he adored. "It's okay," she absently soothed the dog, who was no longer a little puppy.

It felt like an arrow to the heart. Ava hadn't seen him since the rodeo on that cold summer morning.

"This isn't this pair's first trip to the NFR, but it's the first time we've seen Carson since his injury last spring."

The camera shifted to Carson's elbow. He wore a brace.

"That's right. The man suffered a terrible injury early on in the rodeo season and missed nearly two-thirds of it. But then he came back with a bang. He hasn't missed a steer in months. It's incredible."

Ava looked at Bella sharply. That was the first time she'd heard that. She hadn't asked and her daughter hadn't volunteered the information. Bella still took lessons out at Gillian Ranch, although it was more often than not that Flynn, Carson's brother, schooled her these days. That was okay with Ava. Less chance of running into Carson when she dropped Bella off.

"This pair managed to qualify for the NFR in a record three months' time," said the other announcer. "That's remarkable, given that there was a chance Carson would never rope again."

The camera shifted to Shane again. He'd backed his horse into the corner of the box, as she'd learned it was called thanks to Bella. The view changed, zooming out to include Carson, who swung his rope while backing up his horse, too. And despite telling herself she didn't care, her pulse pounded so hard she could feel it throb in her neck.

"Here we go," said the announcer.

Shane nodded. The view changed again, this time including Shane and the steer. Carson's brother only had to swing three times before tossing his rope, Ava gasping as he caught the head, turned him. Ava's hands clenched as Carson swung next.

He caught.

"Would you look at that!" yelled an announcer. "What a way to start off your NFR."

"They did it!" Bella yelled, shooting up from the couch and giving Ava a high five.

"My goodness," said the other announcer. "That was something else. Looks like this will be one of the teams to watch over the next two weeks."

On television, Carson smiled at his brother. Ava couldn't watch anymore.

"Where are you going?" Bella asked with troubled eyes. "The round just started."

"I just need to go upstairs and get something."

She didn't wait to see Bella's reaction. She knew her daughter would understand. She'd tried more times than Ava could count to get her to call Carson before he'd left for the NFR. She'd refused every time, even though it'd disappointed Bella.

She went right to the rocking chair. How many times had she sat on it and thought about where he was and what he was doing? There'd been days, too, when she'd wanted to toss it out the window. Such talent. Didn't he realize she was far more impressed with his ability to mold wood than his talent chasing cows—or steers as she'd now learned they were called.

Ava stroked the soft wooden arms, pulled a blanket she'd tossed over the back around her, staring outside at the twinkling lights in her front yard and at other homes around her.

She missed him.

Lord, she hadn't known it would hurt so badly. When she'd confessed to Bella that she loved him, she'd wondered if it would last. Everything had happened so fast between them, it didn't seem possible to care that deeply in such a short amount of time. But she did. She missed his teasing smiles and his twinkling eyes and the heat in his gaze when he stared down at her. And despite telling herself not to, she felt tears well in her eyes.

He'd chosen rodeo. That was fine. He was gone a lot. It would have been tough to deal with that.

But she loved him. He loved her, too. She closed her eyes, a tear escaping from between her lashes.

She'd fallen in love with a cowboy. Too bad that love wasn't enough to make it all work.

"What's wrong, son?"

Carson stared at the trophy frame that held his brand-new gold-and-silver buckle. "Nothing."

They were in his hotel room, the bright Las Vegas strip visible from outside his window. It didn't impress him. Nothing seemed to impress him these days.

His dad plopped down on a nearby couch. The Gillian family shared a suite, the whole group having gone out to celebrate. He and Reese would join them in a few. Carson had wanted to drop his buckle off in his room.

"You don't look like someone about to win the average at the NFR."

He inhaled again, and he knew his dad would notice, but he didn't care. He felt…empty. This whole time he'd been so focused on making the NFR, he hadn't had time to think. That was good. Ava had kept her distance.

He'd told himself that was probably for the best, too. He wasn't cut out to be a dad. He loved Bella, no doubt about that, but he had goals now. Things to do. Places to go. People to see.

That was what he told himself.

Only now, as he stared down at his buckle in its shadow box, did he realize it meant nothing. The wins. The money. The chance at winning the average, and maybe even the world if his earnings kept going up. None of it meant a hill of beans. Not without Ava.

"You miss her, son?"

Leave it to his dad to read his mind. "Miss who?"

His father shook his head. Carson set the trophy buckle down on the granite counter that separated the kitchen from the living area, next to the other two he'd won during the ten-day competition.

"Don't hand me that. You know who I'm talking about."

He did. Not a day went by that he didn't think about Ava. His longing for her was an ache in his heart.

"She probably doesn't even know I won a round."

"Oh, I think Bella will keep her informed."

Carson nodded. His dad got up from the couch. "I'm proud of you, son," he said, squeezing Carson's arm.

"Thanks, Dad." But even that, his dad's praise— something that meant the world to him—fell flat.

"But I'm not proud of the cowardly way you walked away from that woman."

Carson's head snapped up.

"Bella told me about it the other day. About how she told you that you shouldn't rope. About how you resisted at first. That's why you switched to that new doctor. It wasn't so you could see a specialist. You just didn't want to see Ava anymore."

Carson stuffed his hands into his pockets. "You were the one that said things probably wouldn't work out."

"That doesn't mean I didn't hope." Reese leaned forward. "Damn it, son. I told you that was a hell of a woman. But you walked away from her even though it's pretty damn clear that you're in love."

He didn't want to have this conversation. Not now. "You ready to go eat?" he asked.

"Hear me out." His dad lifted a hand. Carson resisted the urge to walk out anyway. "That woman was the best thing to ever happen to you."

Why did the words sting so much?

"She made you want to do things that I'd only ever hoped you'd do. She helped you to see that you could be better than the person you were before the two of you met. That you could be a dad. That you could care for someone, not just for a night or a couple weeks, but forever. You love her. Still."

Yes, he did. Had wanted to tell her that at least a half dozen times over the phone. He'd held back out of pride.

"You love her and now you realize that none of it, not winning another buckle, not being the best heeler in the nation, not even all the money you've won—none of it means anything without her."

Carson's face began to crumble. It was the oddest sensation to feel his cheeks sag and his lids lower and his mouth tremble as he fought to hold back tears. Wasn't manly to cry.

"Go to her, son. Tell her how you feel. If you don't, I promise you, victory won't be sweet, it'll be hollow and, worse than that, lonely as hell. It always is at the top, especially when you don't have the woman you love by your side."

Chapter 22

"Dr. Moore, please report to the reception counter."

Ava paused, looking up from the X-rays she examined. Compound fracture. Just as she'd thought. The misshapen bend to the man's right wrist had been a dead giveaway, although thankfully it hadn't pierced the skin.

"How bad is it, Doc?"

Ava focused on the man whose X-rays she'd just studied and smiled. At least work kept her busy. She'd slept hardly a wink all night, not after listening to Bella hooting and hollering when it was announced that Shane and Carson had won not only the average, but the world title, too.

"I've seen worse, Mr. Johnson. It's a clean break, though."

"Will you be able to set it?" said a woman who'd been introduced as his wife. Her husband had been riding their ten-year-old's skateboard, and if Ava had a dollar for every fortysomething who'd thought to relive their youth by hopping aboard a kid's toy, she'd be rich.

"Yes. It's a simple break, fortunately. I'll have a nurse give you a local and then I'll pull it back in place."

Mr. Johnson winced. She didn't blame him. It sounded a lot worse than it was, though. One good tug and the bone would be straight again. The man wouldn't feel a thing.

"Dr. Moore, reception desk, please."

"It'll take a little while for the local to kick in, so you might as well make yourself comfortable."

The wife nodded. The man seemed to relax a bit. Ava headed for the door.

"I told you not to get on that thing," she heard Mrs. Johnson hiss. "You're lucky you didn't break your neck."

Ava smiled. It was good to be at work. Good to be away from it all.

She stopped at the nurses' station. "Can you have Nurse Bell administer a local to Mr. Johnson? That wrist will have to be set."

Sally, her head RN, nodded, a strange smile on her face. She'd probably heard the woman's comment from the other side of the curtain, too. "Anything else you'll need?"

"Just the usual. Casting tape. Padding. Maybe a Xanax for the wife."

Sally's smile grew. "Got it. And you were paged to the reception desk."

"Yeah, I heard." She turned away, wondering what they needed. Sometimes her patients stopped by if they couldn't find her at her office. It was a major pain in her rear, but it was part of the job to answer questions even when it pulled her away from the ER.

"There you are," said the pretty brunette who manned Via Del Caballo General's main reception desk. "I was hoping you heard me."

"What's up, Meghan?"

The woman had the biggest smile on her face, making an already attractive face even more pretty. "This just came for you." She handed her a white box with a blue ribbon tied around it. Ava stared at it in surprise.

"What is it?"

"I don't know."

Well, of course she didn't know. She untied the ribbon, lifted the lid…and gasped.

NATIONAL FINALS RODEO
TEAM ROPING—HEELER.

"Is that a buckle?"

She hadn't even noticed Meghan standing. Didn't realize she'd set the shadow box frame down, stepping back as if it might burn her.

"Holy cow. That's Carson Gillian's, isn't it? That was him, wasn't it?" Meghan couldn't contain her excitement. "No wonder he looked so familiar."

Wait. "Carson was here?"

"Yes," Meghan said. "Oh, what does the card say?"

He was here? Ava glanced toward the door. "I don't know," she answered absently. She didn't see his truck in the visitor parking, but she couldn't see the entire parking lot from where she stood.

"It says," said a masculine voice, "'I couldn't have done it without you.'"

It was a sign of how distracted she was that she hadn't heard him approach.

"Love, Carson," he added.

He held roses.

She stood, rooted to the spot. He took a tentative step toward her. She began to move, too. Slowly at first and then faster.

She gave up.

She loved him. Couldn't live without him. She didn't care that he hadn't listened to her at first. That he lived a life on the road. Nothing was worse than being without him. She knew that now. Time had revealed the truth of their love.

"Ava," he said, hugging her tight, swinging her around, the roses crushed against her back, their blooms emitting a heavenly smell.

"I'm so glad you answered that page because I was prepared to go into *An Officer and a Gentleman* mode and march through the hospital hallways until I found you if you hadn't."

He felt so good. Smelled so familiar. Held her so tight. She closed her eyes, part of her wondering if it was really happening, wondering if it might be a dream because there was no way he could have arrived all the way from Las Vegas.

"Wait. What are you doing here?" she asked, leaning back. "Carson, you're going to miss your next go if you don't head back right now."

His smile was all the more heartwarming for the tears she spotted in his eyes. "You saw me last night."

Her eyes blurred suddenly as she stared up at him. "I swore I wouldn't. I told Bella to turn it off, but I couldn't seem to stop myself."

His hand lifted, brushing a tear from her cheek. "Then you know if I keep this up, I could win the whole shebang. The average. The world title."

She nodded. "But only if you turn around and drive back to Vegas right now."

He shook his head. "I'm not going to do it. I'm not going to ride…not unless you're there with me."

She couldn't breathe for a moment, had to look away because until that moment she hadn't thought there was a thing he could say that would top his being there. She realized then she was wrong.

"I can't go with you, Carson. I have patients to attend to. Hell, there's a forty-six-year-old man in there every bit as stupid as you and I need to set his arm in a few minutes."

He shushed her with a finger against her lips. "But you would go, wouldn't you?"

He realized what he was asking her then, although he really should have known by the look on her face. She had to be staring up at him like a love-struck fool.

"I would," she said softly.

"Then it's a good thing I called Dr. Eastman and arranged it all this morning."

She drew back in shock. "What?"

"Look," he said, gently turning her.

In the hospital lobby, lined up three-people thick, was most of the ER staff, smiles on their faces. Some of them started to clap, Nurse Bell giving her the thumbs-up.

And then she felt Carson move. When she turned, it was in time to see him get down on one knee.

"Marry me, Ava," he said. "Come back to Vegas with me and we'll do it together. You and I will conquer the world."

Her eyes began to burn. She didn't want to cry. Not in front of her coworkers, but she couldn't seem to stop herself.

He set her roses down, pulled a ring out of his pocket, flipped open the lid. "Marry me, Ava. Let me prove to you how much I love you for the rest of our lives."

She couldn't stop it then, couldn't hold back the tears any longer. "Well, okay. When you put it that way…"

Which was probably the silliest thing to say to a man who had just asked you to marry him, but she didn't care. The staff clapped harder when Carson stood and slipped a gorgeous emerald-cut diamond on her finger.

"Momma," she heard someone say.

It was Bella. Her daughter ran into her arms.

"I'm so happy for you," she murmured into her chest. Carson held them both tight. "I love you two so much."

"Me, too," Ava sobbed. "Me, too."

They left right then and there, Carson explaining that Nurse Bell had already clocked her out and Dr. Eastman was covering for her. He drove like a bat out of hell to get back to Vegas, and Ava half joked that it would be just their luck to crash on their way to the NFR.

He didn't.

They arrived in plenty of time, the Gillian family welcoming her with open arms when they arrived. And later on, when Shane and Carson roped their final steer of all the go-arounds in record time, she stood with his family afterward, smiling through her tears as she congratulated the second generation of Gillians to win gold buckles.

There were more tears that night when Carson and Shane received their final buckles, not to mention the saddles the two would bring home. And a promise to Bella that she could be her maid of honor. And a promise from Carson that he would curtail his rodeo activities if that was what she wanted. But it wasn't what she wanted. As Ava stood in the arena that night, rodeo fans screaming Carson's and Shane's names, she admitted she could never take that away from him. All she wanted and needed was for him to stand by her side for the rest of her life.

And that was exactly what he did.

Epilogue

There was a festive feeling in the air at Gillian Ranch.

"Wow, look." Bella sat forward in her seat. "Carson put up birthday decorations."

Ava guided the car to its familiar spot in front of the barn. It'd been three months since Carson had asked her to marry him. To this day she got a little misty-eyed when she spotted the ring on her finger. They were hip-deep in wedding preparations, which would take place on the land he'd just purchased from his dad. By next year they'd be married and living in their new house. It was funny, too, because she prided herself on being a feminist, yet when it came to living together, she insisted he stay with his brothers and cousin. She'd make him wait for other things, too, through the last month of their engagement. It'd make things all the more sweet on their wedding night.

"I'll go get Snazzy tacked up." Bella started to bolt from the SUV.

"Wait!" Ava had to grab her daughter by the arm of her pink shirt. "Bella, stop. You're always dashing in there without me. Hold on."

Her daughter's eyes narrowed. Ava tried to keep her expression blank. She didn't want her to know. Didn't want her to guess the surprise.

"Mom, what's going on?"

Dang her sharp-eyed kid. "Nothing."

She slipped out of the SUV before Bella spotted the lie in her eyes. "Come on." She held a hand out to her daughter.

Bella stared up at her strangely. She was ten today, and not a day went by that Ava didn't think about Paul and all that he'd missed out on. Her first day of school. Her first time winning a blue ribbon. And now...

They walked into the barn.

A mass of people called, "Happy birthday!"

Her first horse stood in the aisle.

Bella stopped dead in her tracks. Snazzy's head popped up in surprise, the mare dancing on the cross ties, although that might be because of the hokey birthday hat they'd somehow managed to attach to her halter.

"Oh, Mommy." Her daughter's words carried a tone of reverence. "You didn't." She covered her mouth with her hands, staring at the horse and the people in front of her, before meeting her gaze again. "Is she really mine?"

Carson came out from behind the horse. "She's really yours."

Bella started to cry. Ava started crying, too. Bella ran toward her horse and hugged her. Ava followed in her wake, meeting Carson's eyes.

Paul would have been so proud of his grown-up girl with the big heart. He'd be proud of Ava, too, for finally having the courage to take that first step with Carson. He would have been proud of them all for the way they'd come together as a family.

"Well," said Reese, holding out a bridle to Bella, "you going to ride your new horse?"

"You know I am."

Everyone laughed and Maverick handed her a gift bag. "I think you might need these." Inside was a bunch of brushes that Bella oohed and ahhed over. "Those are yours."

"And this is from us," said his aunt, motioning toward her husband, Bob. She held out a box of some sort.

"See it has your name on the side." She pointed to the BELLA stenciled on it. "It's for your brushes."

"Happy birthday," Reese said, handing her a new saddle pad. Someone else handed her boots for Snazzy's front legs. Bella was soon surrounded by nearly every member of the Gillian family, each of them giving her a horse-related present.

Ava had to take a step back, observing it all.

They would never be alone again.

"I think we did it." Carson pulled her up against him. "I don't think she had any clue what was going on."

"Oh, I think she might have caught on there at the end." She stared up at him. "But it doesn't matter."

He smiled. "No. I guess it doesn't. But you know she's going to want to ride down the aisle on horseback."

"Hmm," she said. "A maid of honor on horseback. It has possibilities."

She laughed. He smiled, and as he so often did, bent to kiss her, and she let him.

Life had never been sweeter. She honestly didn't think anything could top it, but she was wrong.

Six months later when Carson slipped a wedding band on her finger, she topped it with ease. And when, the next year, they moved into their new house on the ranch and she gave birth to a baby boy, she topped that one, too. And so on and so on, right on down the road, because happiness was something that lasted forever after.

* * * * *

SPECIAL EXCERPT FROM

◆ **HARLEQUIN**®

SPECIAL EDITION

*"Brenda Harlen writes couples with such great
chemistry and characters to root for."*
—New York Times *bestselling author Linda Lael Miller*

*The story of committed bachelor Liam Gilmore,
rancher turned innkeeper, and his brand-new manager,
Macy Clayton. She's clearly off-limits, but Liam can't
resist being pulled into her family of adorable triplets!
Is Liam suddenly dreaming of forever after with the
single mom?*

*Read on for a sneak preview of
the next great book in the Match Made in Haven
miniseries,* Claiming the Cowboy's Heart
by Brenda Harlen.

"You kissed me," he reminded her.

"The first time," she acknowledged.

"You kissed me back the second time."

"Has any woman ever not kissed you back?" she
wondered.

"I'm not interested in any other woman right now," he
told her. "I'm only interested in you."

The intensity of his gaze made her belly flutter. "I've
got three kids," she reminded him.

"That's not what's been holding me back."

"What's holding you back?"

"I'm trying to respect our working relationship."

"Yeah, that complicates things," she agreed. Then she finished the wine in her glass and pushed away from the table. "Will you excuse me for a minute? I just want to give my mom a call to check on the kids."

"Of course," he agreed. "But I can't promise the rest of that tart will be there when you get back."

She gave one last, lingering glance at the pastry before she said, "You can finish the tart."

He was tempted by the dessert, but he managed to resist. He didn't know how much longer he could hold out against his attraction to Macy—or if she wanted him to.

Had he crossed a line by flirting with her? She hadn't reacted in a way that suggested she was upset or offended, but she hadn't exactly flirted back, either.

"Is everything okay?" he asked when she returned to the table several minutes later.

She nodded. "I got caught in the middle of an argument."

"With your mom?"

"With myself."

His brows lifted. "Did you win?"

"I hope so," she said.

Then she set an antique key on the table and slid it toward him.

Don't miss
Claiming the Cowboy's Heart *by Brenda Harlen,*
available February 2019 wherever
Harlequin® Special Edition books and ebooks are sold.

www.Harlequin.com

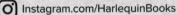
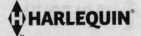

Love Harlequin romance?

DISCOVER.

Be the first to find out about promotions,
news and exclusive content!

 Facebook.com/HarlequinBooks

Twitter.com/HarlequinBooks

Instagram.com/HarlequinBooks

 Pinterest.com/HarlequinBooks

ReaderService.com

EXPLORE.

Sign up for the Harlequin e-newsletter and
download a free book from any series at
TryHarlequin.com.

CONNECT.

Join our Harlequin community to share
your thoughts and connect with other
romance readers!
Facebook.com/groups/HarlequinConnection

**ROMANCE WHEN
YOU NEED IT**

HSOCIAL2018

Earn points on your purchase of new Harlequin books from participating retailers.

Turn your points into **FREE BOOKS** of your choice!

Join for FREE today at
www.HarlequinMyRewards.com.

Harlequin My Rewards is a free program (no fees) without any commitments or obligations.

MYR18